Love your Billionaire Boss

Seduced by Mr. Icecold

Rebecca Baker

Sign up for my newsletter and receive a free romance novel:

https://BookHip.com/LHLBBPG

Chapter 1

Cleo

The bar was loud with cheers, the floor was sticky, and the drink orders kept piling up. Cleo could barely hear as she moved her way around the back of the bar, washing glasses just so she could fill them. She was used to this kind of packed house when there was a game in town. This city went hard for its baseball team.

She looked up to a sea of red and white jerseys clinking their glasses and singing the team's chant. They must have won. She wouldn't know because there was no time to watch. She was not much of a sports girl, anyway. Although she pretended to be to get a job here.

"A round of tequila shots!"

"Two lagers!"

"A Jack and Coke!"

Cleo nodded at the orders being basically barked at her. Sometimes manners went straight out the window on game days. She was used to it, though. She filled the shot glasses, poured the beer, and mixed the cocktail in record time. The patrons took their drinks and turned their backs to watch the game highlights. There was a small lull where Cleo could catch her breath. She leaned against the countertop.

"It's a madhouse today!" Bridget said, nudging her and taking a sip of water.

"You could say that again."

"Hey, at least the tips will be worth it."

Cleo nodded. Bridget was her boss. She had strawberry blonde hair and was tall and slender. Most of the male patrons ogled over her. She had been running the bar for the past year, after she took it over for her father. She was just a few years older than Cleo, but the patrons respected her and loved the bar. It was one of the city's favorite places to catch a game. Cleo had started around the same time Bridget became the owner. They had become good friends.

The bar erupted into cheers, causing Cleo to jump slightly.

"Sounds like they've arrived," said Cleo, glancing at the door.

Bridget nodded and pushed herself away from the counter. She adjusted her top so a little more cleavage showed, and gave Cleo a wink. Cleo shook her head and laughed.

"A girl's gotta do what a girl's gotta do. The players tip very generously," said Bridget as she lifted the counter door and made her way toward the entrance.

Cleo watched as Bridget pushed her way through the crowd to where the team was being swarmed by fans. Most Fridays, the team came here to celebrate if they won the big game.

Another reason why Murphy's was a favorite jaunt for the city. Bridget's father, Conor, had always welcomed the team with open arms and made them feel like home. He was somewhat of a living legend in the city. Conor had known the previous owner of the team through the years. Everyone was so sad when he had fallen ill, which was why Bridget took over the bar, so he could regain his health.

Cleo soaked in the few minutes she had without orders being yelled at her. All the attention was on the players. She watched as Bridget chatted flirtatiously with one of the players. Bridget knew them all by name, but Cleo still hadn't memorized them. There was no reason to. One, she didn't follow the sport. Two, it was Bridget's job to make them feel special and make sure their needs were met.

The bar patrons parted to create a path for the players as Bridget led them to their usual spot. There was a large, round booth at the back of the bar that was specifically for the team on game nights. There were more cheers and pats on the back, and the team finally was able to take a seat in the cushy booth.

"So, what can I get you, boys?" asked Bridget as she leaned over the table and gave them her best dazzling smile.

The players were like cats just lapping her up.

"Beers all around, to start!" said one of the players loudly and giving Bridget a wink.

"You've got it." Bridget made her way back to the bar where Cleo was already lining up glasses on the counter.

"It's going to be a long night," said Bridget, as she began filling the glasses, careful not to add too much foam.

Cleo nodded as she pulled a large tray from the shelf. She began placing the filled glasses of beer on the tray, while mentally remembering orders from the patrons at the bar. She was thankful for her memory because it served her well first as a server, and now a bartender. It was part of the reason Bridget hired her. For her interview, she was basically thrown into the lion's den and was able to keep up with everyone's orders. She may not have been able to make all the drinks, but she knew which drink went to which person. Bridget was impressed and hired her on the spot.

Bridget carried the tray of drinks to the players who all thanked her graciously before they began chugging them down. Cleo watched them for a moment longer before she had to begin making drinks again.

The busy Fridays went on for weeks because the team kept on winning, which meant Cleo worked much later than usual, but she didn't mind because the money was good. It was plenty to pay the rent and also buy the kitchen supplies and ingredients she needed for her real passion, which was baking. When she wasn't behind the bar, she ran a small catering business out of her home just outside of the city. She loved spending her days testing new recipes and baking orders for customers.

However, she wouldn't be able to get much done tomorrow because tonight was looking to be a late one. She would definitely need sleep because Bridget called in sick, which she never did, leaving Cleo in charge. Even though Cleo knew the ropes, she still felt nervous being in charge, especially when she saw the team walk in the bar. The patrons did their normal loud cheers as the team walked through the door.

Cleo glanced at herself in the mirrored wall of the bar. Her chestnut hair could use a wash, so she swooped up her loose curls into a claw clip. A few front tendrils hung and framed her face. She took a deep breath and turned away from her reflection. It was time to play hostess. Cleo wiped her hands on a towel and left her post behind the bar. She had barely spent any time around the players, but she had studied Bridget enough to know what to do. She smoothed her hair and plastered a big smile on her face as she greeted them.

"No Bridget tonight?" asked one of the players.

"Not tonight. Sorry to disappoint, fellas," said Cleo with a small shrug.

"Not a disappointment at all, sweetheart. It's Cleo, right?" asked another player.

"That's right." Cleo gestured to the booth and the players piled in.

"Now what can I get you?" asked Cleo, leaning against the tabletop and trying to look casual.

"Whiskey. All around," said a player.

"Not the usual beer tonight?" She raised an eyebrow.

"Nah, it was a big close call tonight. We need something a little stronger."

Cleo nodded, as if she had any clue what happened in the game.

"I'm Chad, by the way." He winked.

"Nice to meet you, Chad," Cleo said with a close-lipped smile.

Chad nudged the player to his right. "Scooch over, Nico. Let the lady sit." She watched nervously as the players made room for her at the end of the booth. Bridget had sat with the players maybe once before, so this was new, especially for her. She didn't want to get in trouble, but she also didn't want to seem rude. Cleo looked around nervously, but the other bartenders seemed to have the customers handled. She looked at the empty seat a second longer.

"Okay, but only for a moment," said Cleo as she carefully sat next to Chad. She kept her distance and was practically falling off the edge of the booth.

"Thatta girl!" Nico said, raising his glass to her.

Awkwardly, she raised an imaginary glass and clinked it to his, automatically questioning why as soon as she did it. The players laughed and nodded approvingly, which made her feel better about her awkwardness.

"So, what do you do, Cleo?" Chad nudged her.

"Besides serve you?" she replied with a smirk.

Chad let out a laugh. He was handsome, a bit older. Not her type. She wasn't sure if she even had a type. It had been so long since she was interested in anyone. Still, she played along. She was used to being hit on in this line of work.

"Are we *that* bad?" he laughed.

"No, no. I love it here, but when I'm not here, I bake."

"What? Like Betty Crocker?" asked Chad curiously.

"Sure, something like that." She laughed.

"Oh man, Kenny. Did you hear that?" said Chad loudly across the table.

Cleo glanced up at the player Chad was talking to. She caught his eye before quickly looking down at her hands. In the brief look she got at him, he was handsome. Very handsome. His hair was dark brown and tousled in a messy but somehow put together way. As if his hair purposefully fell across his forehead in a perfect swoosh.

"You see, Kenny here has quite the sweet tooth," said Chad, nodding in his direction.

"Is that so?" Cleo couldn't brave looking at him again, so she just smiled and looked back at Chad.

"Mhmm. He could use some sugar in his life." Chad wiggled his eyebrows.

"Oh, shut up," said Kenny, shooting him a look.

Cleo laughed nervously. She didn't sound like herself.

"Well, I had better get back to work. I'll have that whiskey right out." She stood and nodded at the players, being careful not to glance at Kenny, although she could feel his eyes on her.

She backed away from the booth and walked swiftly behind the bar where she took a deep breath. What was happening to her? One look at a guy and she'd lost her wits. She shook her head at herself and began pulling shot glasses

10

from the shelf. She found the high-end whiskey on the top shelf, and began pouring generously. She heard the players laughing loudly, so she quickly snuck a glance in their direction.

They were all immersed in a conversation, except for one who was looking up at her from under his ball cap. Kenny. They locked eyes for a moment before she realized she had poured too much and the whiskey was running onto the tray.

"Oh shoot," Cleo said, breaking eye contact.

"You okay, Cleo?" asked Sarah, another bartender.

"Yeah, yeah. Just making a mess over here." Cleo grabbed a rag and began wiping at the tray.

"You usually have a steady hand," said Sarah curiously, looking from Cleo to the booth of players.

"Was one of the players out of line? I saw you over there." Sarah raised an eyebrow.

"No, no. They were all fine," Cleo assured her.

"Okay, you let me know. Bridget has a no-harassment policy, no matter who it is."

"Thanks, Sarah. But I'm fine. Promise."

Sarah nodded and began mixing a drink in a metal shaker.

Cleo picked up the tray of shots carefully and made her way back to the booth slowly. She didn't trust herself, especially being this close to the stranger that she hadn't spoken one word to.

"Here you go, boys. Top shelf." She set the tray down and the players all reached in to grab their shots.

"Thank you!" they said in almost perfect unison. They took their shots and then whooped and hollered, except for Kenny. He seemed more reserved. More serious. He looked down at the table as if deep in thought. She watched him a little longer, until it was no longer safe and someone would catch her.

"Well, let me know if you need anything else." Cleo nodded and walked away, curious about the silent type at the table.

Chapter 2

Kenny

Kenny sipped slowly on the shot of whiskey, even though the rest of his team was already thinking about their next drink. He wasn't in the partying mood tonight, even though they'd won the big game. It was a close one that had them all on edge until the tenth inning when Nico hit the game-winning ball.

It was Nico who had convinced Kenny to come out tonight. Nico was one of Kenny's best friends and roommates. He was definitely a playboy, and Kenny could be, too, since Sylvie broke up with him two years ago. The breakup still left a bitter taste in Kenny's mouth and a hole in his heart that he couldn't fill, despite the one-night-stands he'd tried.

He hadn't seen it coming. They were high school sweethearts. They went to the same college, and she was at all his home games cheering him on. Everyone said they were going to get married. They even talked about it. He had watched her talk enthusiastically about who her bridesmaids would be and what flowers she would want in her bouquet. He wanted whatever she wanted.

"Where would we go on our honeymoon?" *she asked with her head in his lap, looking up at him expectantly.*

He looked down at her and brushed a strand of blonde hair from her forehead. "Wherever you want. Europe. The Caribbean. Bali. The options are endless."

She leaned up toward him and kissed him before nestling back onto his lap. He watched her blue eyes close, but he knew her mind was fluttering with ideas. She had no idea he had picked a ring out, but was waiting until graduation to propose.

"We'll make it, right?" she asked, her eyes slowly opening and meeting his.

"That's a silly question," he said.

"It's just with my summer internship being across the country…"

"People make long distance work all the time. And those people aren't us. They're normal people. We are Kenny and Sylvie. Inseparable since fifteen." Kenny lowered his forehead to hers.

Sylvie nodded and smiled. "You're right."

And he had been, for the first month of summer when she started her internship on the west coast. They talked every day on the phone and she flew in for his birthday. He missed her, but he threw himself into baseball as a distraction. He was in the gym every day and stayed late after practice. After the second month, the phone calls became less frequent. His calls would often go to voicemail and his texts wouldn't receive responses for hours.

After a few weeks of this, he decided to fly in to surprise her.

He packed a duffel bag and flew four hours, then took a taxi to her apartment, picking up flowers on the way. When he got to her door, he could hear loud music from inside. He knocked. After a little while he knocked again, louder this time.

He heard a man's voice through the door. "Our takeout's here! Will you turn that down?"

Kenny took a few steps back to check the apartment number, and then the door opened to a shirtless man standing in the doorway. He looked to be in his mid-thirties.

"Oh, I'm sorry. I think I have the wrong apartment," said Kenny apologetically.

"Are you delivering for Dragon Palace?" The man eyed his duffle bag.

Kenny shook his head. "Sorry, man."

He turned and took a few steps, pulling his phone out of his pocket to double check the address, when he heard Sylvie's laughter. He turned toward it and saw her come up behind the man and put her arms around him.

"What's the holdup? I'm starving." She kissed the man's neck before her gaze caught on Kenny.

She gasped and released her hold on the man in the doorway.

"Kenny! What are you doing here?" she asked loudly as she tightened the silk robe, which left little to the imagination.

"Sylvie. Who is this?" Kenny asked, clutching the strap of his duffle bag to steady himself.

"Uh...I'm Ben," said the man, confused.

"Ben, as in your boss?" Kenny looked at Sylvie.

"I was going to tell you," said Sylvie softly, looking at the ground.

Kenny felt like he was either going to pass out, throw up, or deck Ben in the face. Instead, he somehow forced his legs to move, and his feet to walk him down the hallway.

"Shit, shit, shit," Sylvie said behind him.

He heard her running after him.

"Kenny! Wait!"

He kept walking.

"I'm sorry, okay? I didn't realize how much I needed to be on my own."

"You don't look like you're on your own," muttered Kenny.

"You know what I mean."

"Do I?" Kenny whipped around and faced her. "It's been you and me for six years. You were my first kiss, my first everything. I didn't know anything else." " I thought that's what made us special."

"It did!" She pleadingly reached for his hand.

"Don't." Kenny glared at her.

"I'm sorry."

"Yeah, me, too." He turned away from her and walked down the stairwell.

It wasn't until he was in a cab riding back to the airport, that he let himself fall apart.

Since then, he hadn't been interested in relationships. His focus was baseball, with the occasional fling to meet his needs. He looked around the bar, but no one caught his eye, except for the bartender. She had curves she didn't know were dangerous, hidden beneath a baggy shirt and a bar apron. It was probably better that way or else the guys would be all over her. For some reason, Kenny felt protective of her and he had barely spoken to her. Maybe it was her smile that had a sadness behind it. He kept stealing glances at her behind the bar.

"Earth to Kenny!" Nico nudged him.

"Sorry, what?" Kenny broke out of his thoughts.

"You haven't even finished your shot."

"Oh, right." Kenny drank the rest and set his shot glass on the table.

"Atta boy."

Kenny shook his head, smiling, and glanced around the table. As much as he liked his teammates, he wasn't close with many of them, besides Nico. They were more like colleagues and party mates than friends. The truth was, Kenny had a hard time trusting many people. And it wasn't just because of Sylvie.

He had recently found out he had a brother, which wasn't a big surprise, as his father had a bit of a reputation back in the day. Kenny had never met his father, but he knew who he was. His mother had told him when he was old enough to understand. His father was a successful businessman in the city, and as unfaithful as they came. The marriage was a façade for all the things he did behind the scenes. One of those things being Kenny's mother.

When she had told him that she was pregnant, Kenny's father offered to pay her off. Not the fairytale ending she was hoping for, she refused. The combination of her pride and her broken heart couldn't accept the money. Even without the money, she never said a word, until she told Kenny when he was thirteen.

The money could have been useful for the two of them. His mother worked three jobs just to pay the rent and keep food on the table. She resented his father for his money, but stood strong in her stance not to ask for help. While he didn't have much growing up, Kenny loved his childhood and his mother fiercely.

While finding out he had a brother wasn't a surprise, finding out it was someone he knew was not something Kenny was prepared for. It turned out that his brother, Nate, was a business partner to the team's owner, Jonas. Nate must have been unaware because he hadn't said anything or approached Kenny about it. It was probably better that way, although Kenny couldn't help feeling some resentment toward his older brother. The brother his father actually wanted and raised.

"Hey, hey, hey." A voice broke through Kenny's thoughts. He looked up and saw his best friend, Justin.

"Hey, man. Make some room, guys."

The team scooched in and Justin eased himself into the booth, letting out a sigh.

"Did you just get in?" asked Kenny.

"About an hour ago. Sorry I missed the game." Justin loosened his tie.

"No worries, man. We still on for tomorrow?" Kenny asked.

"Yes. Nine a.m. at your place?"

Kenny nodded. They had set up this meeting last week to go over Kenny's investments. Justin was his advisor and often came in town from New York on business. He had been a godsend since Kenny was drafted and had more money than he knew what to do with. Growing up with less than most, Kenny was determined to be smart with his money and help take care of his mother. He wanted to prove he didn't need his father.

"Should we order another round of drinks, boys?" Nico asked.

"Bartender!" Chad shouted.

Kenny glanced at the bar and watched as she seemed to literally put a smile on her face. He had the sudden urge to see what a genuine smile looked like, and wondered if he could be the one to give her one.

She ducked under the bar counter door and walked over to their booth, keeping her eyes on the floor. It wasn't until she was at the table that she looked up. She looked at everyone except Kenny, which made him feel the slightest tinge of insecurity.

"Would you boys like another round?" she asked, tucking a strand of hair behind her ear.

"Let's do another round of shots and a round of the pale ale," said Chad, flashing a smile.

"I'm on it." She turned toward the bar, but quickly snuck in a glance at Kenny that wasn't expecting. He quickly looked down.

What was wrong with him? Nerves weren't his thing. Especially with women.

"Where's Bridget?" Justin asked curiously.

Nico shrugged.

Kenny, forgetting the pretty bartender's name, saw his opportunity. "Yeah, what's our bartender's name again?"

"Katie? Connie? Carrie?" Chad started listing off names.

"No, no. It's something you don't hear very often," said Nico, squinting his eyes in thought.

Just then, she plopped a tray onto the table and started passing out drinks. Kenny watched as she focused on her work. She was different from Bridget. She didn't seem to care who they were and treated every customer the same. He liked that. He was used to girls throwing themselves at him, which made it easy to take them home, but not anything more than that.

"Hey, honey," said Chad.

"Hmm?" she asked, as she continued passing out the drinks.

"What's your name again? Our boy Kenny was asking." Chad nodded toward Kenny, who felt himself sink into his seat. He was embarrassed Chad had put him on the spot like that.

She met his eye for a second and furrowed her brows slightly. She paused before answering. "It's Cleo."

Kenny nodded and looked down at the table.

She slid him his drinks and picked up her tray before turning. "Let me know if you need anything else," she called behind her.

When Kenny felt it was safe to look, he watched as she walked away. She was like a magnet, and his eyes couldn't help follow where she was. He needed a distraction from whatever intrigue he had for this stranger. He took his shot and gulped down his beer.

"Well, well, well. Look who showed up to the party!" said Nico, slapping him on the back. The rest of the table cheered and followed suit.

"Should I text those girls from last weekend?" asked Nico, pulling out his phone.

"Sure, but let's hop bars tonight. Have them meet us at the next one," said Kenny. As much as he wanted a distraction from the pretty bartender named Cleo, for some reason he didn't want her to see.

Chapter 3

Cleo

Sunday morning, Cleo slid the covers off and sat up, stretching her arms above her head. She checked her phone for the time. It was just past 9 a.m. She yawned as she swung her feet to the floor and slid on her fuzzy slippers. As tired as she was, she needed to get up.

It had been a long night at the bar. Bridget took another night off to recover from her cold, which meant Cleo was in charge again. She was thankful it wasn't a game night because she didn't know if she could handle that type of crowd again. Although, she wouldn't be too upset to see that one player. Kenny.

She couldn't get him out of her head. She wasn't sure if it was his quiet mannerisms, or his warm brown eyes, or because he seemed different from the rest of his team. Cloe kept thinking of the moments they locked eyes. It didn't last long, but the power those few seconds held over her was unusual.

She made her way to the bathroom to brush her teeth and wash her face. As she dried off with a towel, she heard her phone ding from her nightstand. She walked over and slid it unlocked. It was a text.

Elle: *I'll be over in fifteen minutes. I'm hungry* □

Cleo laughed to herself. Elle was her best friend and taste tester in the kitchen. At least once a week she came to "assist" Cleo in the kitchen, although she didn't do much besides talk and sneak a few tastes. Cleo didn't mind, though. She enjoyed the company. Despite working in a bar filled with people, it could really feel quite lonely.

Cleo slid on some comfy sweats and made her way downstairs to the kitchen to make a pot of coffee. She needed the caffeine—she had a lot of baking ahead. She had been perfecting her recipes for the past few weeks in order to get her foot in the door at one of the city's cafés. Up until now, she had just baked for friends and family, and a few small local events. Now she felt like was ready to take the leap into making it an actual business.

The coffee made, Cleo poured herself a steaming cup and pulled her recipe book from the shelf. She began flipping through the pages to choose which recipes she would bake today. She had just decided on cinnamon rolls, muffins, and streusels when the doorbell rang.

She walked to the door and opened it to find Elle standing there with a big smile. Cleo hugged her tightly and waved her inside.

Elle sniffed around and frowned slightly. "I don't smell anything scrumptious."

"That's because I haven't started yet." Cleo laughed.

"But I'm starving," said Elle dramatically.

"I'm sure I have some leftover blueberry muffins."

"Phew." Elle wiped imaginary sweat from her forehead.

"What would you do without me?"

"I have no idea."

Cleo shook her head and smiled as she pulled out a container full of blueberry muffins she had baked a few days ago. She placed one on a plate and warmed it in the microwave. Elle took the plate from her graciously and took a large bite.

Her eyes fluttered closed. "Mmmmm. These are heavenly."

Cleo smiled. There was no better feeling than watching someone enjoy what she made.

"Seriously, Cleo! These need to be in every café. You have a gift, my friend."

"I'm actually going to shop myself out in a few days. I'm hoping one of the city's cafés bite. Literally."

Elle laughed. "They will. They have to."

Cleo nodded hopefully before letting out a big yawn. She reached for her cup of coffee and took a long sip.

"Long night?" Elle raised an eyebrow.

"I didn't get out of there until four a.m."

"Sheesh, girl."

"I know. I keep telling myself it's not forever. Besides, I really like Bridget."

"How is she feeling, by the way?" asked Elle, as she took another bite of her muffin.

"She's feeling better. She should be back running things tonight."

Elle nodded. "Good, good. And now you have the next few days to focus on this." She waved around the kitchen. "So, what are we making today?"

Cleo smiled. "*I* am making maple cinnamon rolls, coffee cake muffins, and strawberry cream cheese strudels."

"Hey now. I assist. Kind of. That all sounds delicious."

"Mhmm," said Cleo sarcastically, as she began sorting through ingredients in her pantry.

For the next hour she mixed ingredients meticulously, every once in a while tasting the different batters and dough. Elle knew the right times to talk, and when to be quiet to let Cleo focus. They had known each other long enough to understand each other's body language and mannerisms by heart.

As kids, they had lived across the street from one another. Cleo had a treehouse they would camp out in with their pre-teen magazine posters taped to the walls and their crushes' names carved into the wood. Every weekend, they would have sleepovers at each other's houses. They were in every class together. Even though they couldn't stop talking, the teachers never separated them.

They were there for each other through their first boyfriends and breakups, Elle's parents divorcing, and the untimely death of Cleo's grandmother. They were the definition of best friends, and even though they were accepted at different colleges, they remained close. Making a pact, they promised they would end up in the same city after graduation, which ended up being Boston.

"Okay, the strudels are done. The muffins are going in the oven. The cinnamon rolls have to proof for a while," said Cleo as she studied her recipe book for a minute. When she was sure of herself, she poured another cup of coffee and took a seat at the kitchen table. Elle hopped off the counter and took the seat across from her.

"Soooo..." said Elle, giving Cleo a small smirk.

"I know that look."

"What look?" Elle shrugged innocently.

"The look before you ask, 'are you seeing anyone?'"

"Well, are you?" Elle took a sip of coffee.

"Not since the last time you asked, which was what? Two days ago."

Elle laughed.

Cleo shook her head before taking another sip of coffee. She had no time to date. Between working at the bar and baking on her days off, she was too tired to even toy with the idea. Plus, the last date she went on was a disaster. And of course, it was Elle's idea.

Elle had set her up with one of her office coworkers. She had seen him in the copy room and thought he was kind of cute. After a quick, casual conversation, she gave him Cleo's number. She had told an annoyed Cleo that she thought it would be better to ask for forgiveness than permission.

Cleo accepted his invitation to dinner on her night off from the bar. She met him at a fancy restaurant he chose that was in the heart of the city. The night started out rocky when he showed up twenty minutes late. Since it was her first date since she moved to Boston, she let it slide in hopes it would go up from there. Instead, it did the opposite. He was on his phone most of the time. He claimed he forgot his wallet, although she could have sworn he walked in holding one. At the end of the night, he basically made out with her cheek when she turned her head at his advances.

"You know...there's a new guy at my—" Elle started.

Cleo held up her hand. "Nope. No way. What did I tell you after the last time?"

"Oh, come on! I didn't know it was going to be the date from hell."

"Never again." Cleo shook her head.

"Fiiiiine." Elle threw her head back dramatically.

"Why don't you just focus on *your* relationship?"

"Booooring," groaned Elle.

"Oh, come on. You love Brad."

"I do, I do. We're just like an old married couple. I need some spice, so I'm trying to live through you."

"Well, there's some cinnamon in the cabinet." Cleo nodded toward the kitchen.

"Oh, shut up." Elle laughed. "I mean it, Cleo. You've got to get out there."

Cleo shrugged.

"You work in one of the most popular bars in the city. You're surrounded by men four nights a week. You could easily have your pick."

"Yeah, right. Plus, they're too busy shouting out drink orders or watching the game to actually talk to me."

"Well, what about the players? I know they go in there almost every home game night."

"What about them?"

Elle sat back in her chair, exasperated. "Oh, I don't know. Tight pants. Nice butts. Even nicer paychecks."

Cleo laughed out loud. "You're ridiculous."

"I'm serious. Why don't you talk to them?"

Cleo thought about telling her about Kenny from the other night, but she knew better. Elle would never leave her alone about it. She'd probably show up at the bar next home game and embarrass Cleo. She had good intentions, but she could be a little much sometimes.

"Guys like that don't like girls like me," said Cleo softly.

"Girl, have you seen yourself? You're beautiful. You bake. You know how to make a mean drink. Any guy would be lucky to be with a girl like you."

Cleo shrugged. "Either way. I just want to focus on my baking."

"You're an old lady."

The oven timer went off. Cleo internally sighed with relief. Perfect timing. She wasn't sure how much more she could fend off Elle. Cleo stood from her chair and put on her oven mitts. She pulled the muffins out and placed them on a cooling rack, as the kitchen filled with a warm, spicy, and sweet aroma. This was her happy place.

After a successful Sunday of baking, Cleo spent most of the day in bed catching up on sleeping and then mapping out the different cafés she was going to visit in the coming days. Her plan was to take each one a basket of assorted goods for them to sample, and hopefully that would act as her résumé. The plan was to grow by word of mouth and eventually open her own bakery. It was going to take time, which was why she had better start now.

On Monday in the late afternoon, she packed up a small container of cinnamon rolls and headed to Murphy's. It was her night off, but she wanted to bring Bridget a treat since she had been sick.

When she opened the door, she saw maybe five people sitting around the bar.

Bridget saw her and momentarily looked confused. "It's your night off!" she called out.

"I know, I know. I thought I'd bring you a treat since you've been feeling crummy."

Bridget eyed the container as Cleo approached. "Please tell me those are cinnamon rolls."

Cleo nodded and set them on the countertop. Bridget came around the bar and gave her a hug before plopping down on a barstool. Cleo looked around.

"Sit, sit. It's dead in here," Bridget insisted as she took off the lid and pulled out a cinnamon roll.

Cleo sat down next to her and watched as Bridget took a big bite.

"Mmmm." Her eyes rolled to the back of her head. "What is that frosting?"

"Maple." Cleo smiled.

"I swear. You are the best baker in the city."

"We'll see. The jury's still out."

"I'm serious." Bridget took another bite. "I'm going to miss you when you leave this place to open your dream bakery."

"You might be stuck with me," said Cleo softly, with a sad smile.

"Have a little faith, girl." Bridget squeezed her hand reassuringly.

Cleo nodded. She was going to miss this place if she ever got her dream up and running.

Chapter 4

Kenny

"You're going to have to push harder," said Kenny's trainer.

Kenny panted as he upped the speed on the treadmill and sprinted even faster, beads of sweat rolling down his forehead. His trainer gave him a look of satisfaction before jotting some notes down on his clipboard. After a minute, he gave Kenny some relief by turning down the speed. Kenny rested his head on the treadmill's dash and caught his breath before drinking some water. His trainer handed him a towel.

"You're trying to kill me," said Kenny between breaths.

"Best time yet," his trainer said, patting him on the back.

Kenny nodded before making his way to the locker room to shower. He spotted the team's owner, Jonas, leaning against the wall. It was rare he came to check on the team during their workouts, so Kenny was glad he had performed well. He gave Jonas a nod as he passed by.

He didn't talk much to Jonas. He was always a little intimidated by the guy, but Jonas was also Nate's business partner. Nate, as in Kenny's long-lost brother. With everything that had come to light, Kenny kept his head down. He did what he needed to on the field and in the gym, and that got him by.

His phone dinged as he turned on the shower. It was a text from Justin: *Are we still on for lunch?*

Yeah, I'm just wrapping up at the gym. What are you feeling?

Anything, just as long as the place is low key.

Got it. I'll text you the address.

Kenny thought for a moment before typing in an address and hitting send. He knew of just the place. A little café on Newbury that was only open for breakfast and lunch. He often took his mom there. She liked it because it was calm and quiet, a little escape from the city. Definitely low key.

Justin was well known in the city. Well known in the country, actually. He was a billionaire and a leader in the tech industry. He had worked alongside his father for years before eventually taking over the company when his father retired. For being as wealthy as he was, Justin was humble. While he enjoyed some finer things, he also enjoyed the little things, which Kenny admired him for.

They met in college. Kenny was there on a baseball scholarship. There was no other way he would be able to afford it. Justin was his assigned dormmate. They hit it off right away and had been best friends ever since.

Kenny hopped in the steaming shower, which felt great for his sore muscles. Once he was finished, he dried off and put on jeans and a white tee. He grabbed his leather jacket from his locker and scheduled an Uber for pickup.

"Hey, man."

Kenny saw his teammate, Kev, walk into the locker room. "Hey, Kev. What's up?"

"Just beat your time." Kev smirked.

Kenny turned and closed his locker, rolling his eyes. Everything was a competition with Kev. He wasn't exactly a team player.

"Congrats."

"Couldn't have you showing me up in front of the boss man."

"I didn't even notice Jonas was there," said Kenny nonchalantly.

"Then you must have missed his bombshell wife, too. I'd like to bring her in here and show her a thing or two." Kev nodded toward the showers.

Kenny shook his head. "Dude, show some respect. She's pregnant."

"I've got a thing for MILFs."

"I'm heading out," said Kenny, ignoring him.

Kev smirked as Kenny passed him and pushed open the door. He jogged downstairs and saw his Uber pull up. He rode the ten minutes to the café and headed inside. Most of the tables were full, but it was quiet. He spotted Justin at a booth by the window.

Kenny took a seat across from him. "Hey, man. Have you been here long?"

"Nah, just got here," said Justin as he picked up his menu.

They both ordered a Reuben and fries, which came out quickly. Kenny took a mouthwatering bite and watched Justin do the same.

"Dude," said Justin, his eyes looking down at his sandwich.

"Right?" Kenny nodded in approval.

"This is the best sandwich I've ever had."

"I know."

"How did you find this place?"

"My mom did, actually."

"How is she doing?"

"She's good."

"Even with the whole Nate thing?" Justin eyed him cautiously.

"She refuses to talk about it." Kenny shrugged.

Justin was the only one who knew about Nate being Kenny's long-lost brother. When Kenny put the pieces together, he had initially gone to his mother, but she was too bitter to confide in. As much as he loved his mother, she could be so stubborn sometimes, especially when it came to talking about the past.

"Do you think he has any idea?" asked Justin, taking a bite of a fry.

Kenny shrugged.

"Wait, even the fries are delicious?" Justin studied the fry in surprise.

Kenny laughed.

"But really, man. This is a lot to bottle up, especially when he's in the industry. Hell, he's your owner's business partner."

"I know, I know. I'm trying my best to just focus on the game."

Just then, the bell to the café rang and Kenny saw the girl from the bar. Cleo. She was wearing a pink strapless dress with small white flowers. Her hair was twisted into a low bun, but wavy strands of her chestnut hair framed her face. She looked different from in the bar. Maybe it was because he was seeing her in the daylight, and not in the dimmed light of Murphy's. She still had that same sad smile.

He watched curiously as she took a deep breath and put on a bigger smile that couldn't hide her nerves. She carried a small brown basket and walked slowly up to the counter. She had white high-top sneakers on, which Kenny loved. He liked her style. She stood at the counter for a moment, rocking back on her heels. Her cheeks were rosy and her lips were painted with a gloss to match. She was even more beautiful than he remembered.

Eventually, she rang the bell on the counter and smoothed out her dress, waiting.

Justin cleared his throat. "Looks like you're focused on more than the game."

Kenny looked away from Cleo and back to Justin, who was smirking at him.

"Who is she?" asked Justin, raising his eyebrows and looking in her direction.

"Who?" asked Kenny innocently, taking another bite of his sandwich.

"Hmm." Justin tapped his cheek with his finger, as if he was thinking really hard. "The brunette with the killer curves and the pink pout that checks off your exact type."

Kenny laughed. "Her name is Cleo. She was our bartender the other night. Remember?"

Justin glanced over at Cleo waiting patiently at the counter. He studied her for a moment. "Really?"

"Okay, stop looking," said Kenny under his breath.

"She looks different when she's not in a T-shirt and jeans."

Kenny nodded, taking a sip of water and stealing another glance. Justin was doing the same.

"Seriously, stop looking at her. You're making it obvious." Kenny kicked him underneath the table.

"Ouch!" said Justin loudly, causing a few customers to look over. Thankfully, Cleo didn't.

"Will you shut up?" whispered Kenny, sinking into the booth.

"Why don't you go talk to her?" Justin leaned down to rub his shin.

"What? No. Besides, she's busy."

And she was. A man from the kitchen had come out to greet her. He was wiping his hands on his apron and eyeing the basket in her hands warily. He must have been the owner. Curious, Kenny tried to eavesdrop without looking too obvious. He was thankful that the man led her to the bar top, which was close enough to hear, but not close enough for her to notice him.

She set her basket on the counter and took a seat on one of the stools next to the man.

"So what can I do for you, young lady?" asked the man.

"I'm Cleo. Cleo Aston. Thank you for taking the time to speak with me."

"Paul."

Cleo nodded before continuing. "So, I'm a baker. I mostly bake out of my home, but I want to get my foot in the door at some of the city's smaller cafés."

"Do you have any training?"

"Well, no, but I'm confident in what I bring to the table."

Paul nodded toward the basket. "What's in there?"

"I brought some samples for you to try. There's cinnamon rolls, muffins, and strudels." Cleo began unwrapping the pastries.

Paul took a bite of each one, taking his time in between. Cleo watched him hopefully, and Kenny couldn't help but do the same. He was internally rooting for her.

After a few minutes of bites and silence, Paul turned toward her. "Look, sweetheart. These are good, don't get me wrong. But I just don't know if they're good enough to be sold here."

"I can bake something else. Anything you'd like." Cleo looked at him intently.

"I'm sorry. We aren't looking for new bakers at this time."

Cleo nodded politely before standing up from her seat. "Thank you for your time." She held out her hand.

Paul shook it gently before heading back to the kitchen.

Kenny watched as Cleo carefully grabbed her basket and let out a deep breath. She looked down at her feet and shook her head. Kenny could feel her dejection and it made his heart hurt for her. She must have felt his eyes on her because she looked up just then. She studied him for a moment before registering who he was. Quickly, she looked away and walked out the door.

"That was rough to watch," said Justin, finishing the last of his sandwich.

Kenny nodded.

"So she's a baker, moonlighting as a bartender?"

"I guess so."

"So, she's a triple threat?"

Kenny eyed Justin curiously as he held up three fingers. "Baker, bartender, bombshell."

Kenny let out a quiet laugh.

"What's stopping you, man?" asked Justin, nodding toward the door.

"You saw what just happened. This would not be a good time."

"With you, there's never a good time."

Kenny shot Justin a look.

"Come on, man. Ever since Sylvie, you've closed yourself off," said Justin warily.

"That's not true."

"The occasional one-night-stand doesn't count."

"It gets me by." Kenny shrugged, taking another bite of his sandwich. "And what about *you?*"

"What about me?"

"I don't see you settling down."

"I'm busy. Plus, I never know if women have the right intentions."

Kenny nodded understandingly. Justin had had a few relationships in the past, but eventually the women showed their true colors. They were always asking for more. More vacations. More jewelry. More designer bags. They didn't love him, they loved his money.

"Maybe you should try a change of scenery," said Kenny, glancing around.

"What? You mean Boston?"

"Yeah, why not? You're here on business every other week, and you could really work from anywhere now that everything is remote."

Justin seemed to think about it for a moment, looking outside the window to the busy sidewalks and street.

"I never thought about coming back here," he said pensively.

"It might be good for you. Away from the bigger city, away from the expectations, away from the women."

"It would be nice to stand on my own a little more without my father breathing down my neck. I swear, you'd think he never retired. I love him, but the man's meticulous."

"Well, think about it. It'd be nice to have my best friend here again."

Justin nodded. "It would be nice to have this sandwich on a weekly basis."

Kenny laughed. "You would take a nice moment and make it about food."

"If I think about moving to Boston, then you have to think about asking that girl out."

"I'll think about it." Kenny lied, even though deep down he kind of wanted to.

Chapter 5

Cleo

Cleo could not have gotten out of the café fast enough. Not only did she face the humiliation of being turned down by the owner, but it was in front of that cute baseball player. Why did he have to be there?

She brushed that part of the humiliation aside and looked down in defeat at the basket of pastries in her hands. She shook her head. She was an embarrassment, walking into one of the city's cafés like little red riding hood peddling goods. But she didn't know any other way of marketing herself.

"Maybe I should just go back to Indiana," she whispered to herself as she walked to her car. There were thirty minutes left on the meter, enough time to try another café, but she didn't think she could handle any more rejection. She had tried five cafés today, and no one was interested. She began to doubt herself and had no confidence left to continue on this venture.

Cleo unlocked the door to her car and slid into the driver's seat, setting the basket next to her in the passenger seat. She leaned her head back and let out a long sigh. She closed her eyes for a moment and wondered if her dreams were too big. Why did she think Boston would be the place where she would get her big break?

She opened her eyes and looked out the window at the café. Just then she saw Kenny heading out the door. She slunk down in her seat in fear he might see her. She could only handle so much embarrassment for one day. Still, she couldn't keep her eyes off him. His brown hair fell messily, but perfectly, against his forehead. He wore a white T-shirt, slim jeans, and a black leather jacket. He was effortlessly good-looking.

She watched as his friend followed behind him. They exchanged a few words and pats on the back before heading different directions on the sidewalk. She wondered if he had recognized her from the bar. She knew he most likely did, but had a faint hope that maybe daylight and a nice dress disguised her. Watching, she waited as he turned a corner, out of sight, before she sat up straight.

Her phone vibrated in her bag and she fished around until she found it. It was a text from Elle: *How did it go?*

It didn't.

Oh no. That bad?

I don't think I'm cut out for this.

Stop. Cleo. Head over to my office for a hug. Plus, I have a sweet tooth ;)

K. Be there in ten.

Cleo clicked her phone to lock, and threw it on the seat. Elle would be just the person to cheer her up. She couldn't dwell on the day for too long, anyway. She had to work in a few hours. Thankfully, there wasn't a game today and it would probably be a slow night. Just what she needed.

Putting her car into drive, she turned on some old school rock to lift her mood. She rolled the windows down and sang to the music. By the time Cleo pulled up to Elle's office building, she was already feeling better. She waved to the parking attendant who recognized her immediately.

"Cleo! It's good to see you."

"Good to see you, Al." Cleo smiled at him.

He peeked in her car and eyed the basket. "Any chance you have an extra for your favorite attendant?"

"You know it." Cleo reached into the basket and pulled out a raspberry and goat cheese strudel. She handed it to Al and watched as he unwrapped it and took a quick bite. A smile spread across his face.

"This is good, Cleo. Really good." He inspected the pastry and took another bite.

"Thank you, Al," she said appreciatively. He didn't know how much she needed that.

"Tell Elle hello for me!" Al hit a button and the arm lifted slowly.

"Thank you." Cleo nodded as she drove down into the parking garage. She parked and grabbed the basket of pastries, planning to just leave them with Elle. Seeing leftovers would just be reminders of her failures from the day.

She rode the elevator up to Elle's floor. When the doors opened, she stepped out and ran right into someone, causing her to drop her basket. "Sorry!" she said, as she knelt down and began picking up the individually wrapped pastries. Whoever she had run into didn't bother to help. Cleo stood up and was face to face with the bad date Elle had set her up with.

"Oh," she said, trying to hide her annoyance.

"Hey…Carrie," he said.

"It's Cleo. How are you, Cole?"

"Shit, sorry. I'm good, I'm good. Heading to lunch."

"Mmm." Cleo looked around, desperate for Elle, or anyone, to come save her from this awkward situation.

"I never heard from you after our date…"

"Right. Uh… I, uh…"

"She's seeing someone, Cole." Cleo heard Elle's voice approaching and gave a little sigh of relief.

"Is that so?" asked Cole.

Cleo nodded and tried to look convincing.

"Yep. He's a baseball player. An all-star." Elle looped her arm through Cleo's and led her down the hallway to her office.

"Thank you." Cleo let out a sigh of relief.

Elle giggled. "Did you see his face when I told him you were dating an MLB player?"

Cleo shook her head. "You really are pushing for that, aren't you?"

Elle shrugged innocently. "Do I need to list the reasons again?"

"Please don't," groaned Cleo.

Elle laughed as she pushed open the door to her office and took a seat at her desk. Cleo plopped down in the leather chair across from her and set the basket on the desk, shoving it toward her best friend. She leaned back and let her head fall back so she was looking up at the ceiling.

"So, what happened?" asked Elle.

"Not one café was interested. The last one said, I might not be 'good enough'." Cleo raised her fingers and made air quotations.

"Bullshit," said Elle.

Cleo sat up and shrugged. "Maybe he's right. Maybe my small-town dreams are too big for the big city."

"It was just an off day."

"Elle, I tried five different bakeries."

"So? Try five more. Hell, try fifty more. I know you're good. Anyone who knows you

48

knows how much heart you put into your baking."

Cleo nodded, but was unconvinced.

Elle pulled the basket toward her and pulled out a muffin. She unwrapped it and inhaled.

"Banana nut. My favorite." She took a big bite and sat back in her chair, closing her eyes and shaking her head. "If no one wanted you after trying *this*, then they don't deserve you. Just watch, I'll put these in the breakroom and they'll be gone before you know it."

"Please do. I can't bear to take them home."

"Done. Leave a business card. These big wigs' wives are always hosting parties."

Cleo fished around her bag for a card and slid it over to Elle. She checked her phone for the time. She had to be at the bar in two hours and still had to go home to clean her kitchen and get ready. "I better go."

Elle stood from her desk and gave her a big hug.

"Don't you dare think you should go back to Indiana. You were made for this and the city needs you. It just doesn't know it yet."

Cleo felt her eyes tear up as she squeezed Elle before letting her go. "Thanks, Elle."

She walked down the hallway toward the elevators, thankful that she didn't have another run-in with the date from hell.

Back home, she washed the dishes and wiped down the counters. She was happy to have the next few days off from baking, since she'd be working late nights at the bar. As much as she loved being in the kitchen, she didn't feel very inspired at the moment. After the kitchen was clean, she changed into her favorite pair of jeans and a tank top that read *Murphy's* across the chest. Her hair still fell in loose curls, so she left it down. She had actually gotten ready for her makeshift job interviews today, and she didn't want to let it go to waste.

When she arrived at the bar, it was surprisingly crowded for 4 p.m. As she clocked in, Bridget came up and greeted her.

"Hey, girl. Looks like we're in for a busy night."

Cleo looked around. "Yeah, what's up with that? There's no game tonight."

"No, but our team's rival lost a big game tonight. Looks like we have a good chance of advancing to the playoffs."

Cleo nodded as if she had any idea about the playoffs.

Bridget eyed her curiously. "You look different. Is that makeup?"

"Long story." Cleo put on her apron.

"Bridget! Can we get a round of those long islands I love so much?" a customer shouted from across the bar.

Bridget nodded and began pulling glasses. "Well, you look smokin', Cleo."

"Thanks, Bridget."

Over the next couple of hours, more and more customers came through the doors of the bar. Cleo could barely catch her breath, but she was thankful for the distraction from the day she had. By 9 p.m., the bar was full. Every seat was taken and people still kept flooding in. They didn't seem to mind standing.

Just then, there were shouts from the doors of the bar. Bridget looked up anxiously as if she was expecting trouble, but then she saw the team walk in. She let out an audible sigh of relief as Cleo sucked in a breath. She was not expecting them tonight. Not on their night off. She was not wanting to see Kenny again. Not after this afternoon.

"Well, this is unexpected." Bridget wiped her hands on a clean towel. "You got the bar?"

Cleo nodded and Bridget walked toward the doors to do her usual hostessing gig with the team. Cleo continued drying glasses and kept her eyes down as to not look too eager to see if Kenny was among his teammates.

"Hello, beautiful."

She looked up suddenly to see a younger man leaning drunkenly against the counter.

"Mm. Hello. What can I get you?"

"Hmm." He looked her up and down slowly, making her feel slightly uncomfortable. "What's your drink?" he asked.

"Water." Cleo held up her water bottle and gave it a little swirl before setting it back down on the counter.

"Boooring. Take a shot with me."

"I'm working."

"Come on, just one shot." He reached over the counter and grabbed two shot glasses.

"I can't have you reaching back here." Cleo looked around for Bridget for help.

"Oh, come on, don't be such a stiff." The man was swaying at this point.

"Maybe I should get you some water," she offered.

"Aww, are you trying to take care of me, sweetheart?" He reached over the counter as if to touch her face, and she quickly stepped backward.

"Hey. Back off," yelled Bridget, stepping next to Cleo. She waved toward the front doors and signaled for security. They briskly walked over and took the man out by his arms.

Cleo leaned against the back counter, watching as the creep was taken out. When he was out the doors, she felt someone watching her. She glanced around and locked eyes with Kenny. His lips were closed and his jaw was tight. He looked angry. Cleo couldn't help but think it was because of what had just happened to her, as if he was protective.

"You okay?" asked Bridget, shaking her head.

"Yeah, I'm fine. Thanks," said Cleo.

Bridget nodded. "Can you get a tray of shots for the players? Whiskey. I've got to go deal with that asshole."

"Sure." Cleo felt nervousness wash over her. She filled a tray of shot glasses and carefully placed it on her palm. She took in a breath as she walked toward their booth.

Chapter 6

Kenny

Kenny sat at the booth, passing his almost full drink back and forth between his hands. It took some convincing to come out tonight with the team. They usually didn't go out on non-game days. He would have much rather stayed home with takeout and a movie. Justin had convinced him to come out though. He was only in town for another day.

"Are you going to drink that or continue to play air hockey with it?" asked Justin, raising an eyebrow at Kenny's full glass.

"I came out, didn't I? I didn't say I was going to go wild." Kenny shrugged.

"What's up with you?"

"Nothing. Just tired."

And he was. He was tapped out socially and needed some alone time to refill his stores. The team was fun and all, but he spent so much time with them that it was nice to have a break sometimes.

The plus side to coming out tonight was seeing Cleo again. She had hardly looked at him all night, not since that jerk was being pushy with her. When Kenny saw the guy reach over the counter to touch her, he saw red. His cheeks were surely flushed with anger, but he tried to swallow it down. Instead, he clenched his fists under the table. He didn't even realize he was staring at her, until she locked eyes with him briefly.

"Now there's a guy who takes initiative," Kev had said as he watched the guy being thrown out by security.

"That guy's a creep," said Nico, shaking his head.

"So is Kev," said Kenny under his breath. He didn't like the guy, and tried to keep his distance. On the field or out in social gatherings, Kenny was cordial, but didn't go out of his way to be friendly.

"What was that?" Kev snapped, looking at Kenny sharply.

"Hmm?" Kenny raised his eyebrows innocently before taking a drink.

Just then, Bridget came up and leaned casually against the side of the booth. "Sorry about the commotion, boys."

"No apologies necessary, Bridget. By the way, it's good to have you back," said Chad, flashing a smile. It was no surprise to anyone that he had a thing for her.

She smiled and gave Chad a nod. "Well, let me know if you need anything." She pushed off from the booth and walked back toward the bar.

Chad let out an airy whistle. "You think papa Murphy would let me take his daughter out?"

"Doubtful," said Nico. "Now, can we get back to the party?"

"What party?" asked Kenny, taking a sip of his beer.

"Hello? Earth to Kenny. We've been talking about throwing a party for Mae."

"Oh, right."

Justin gave him a knowing smile before looking at Cleo, who was busy behind the bar. Kenny shook his head at him as if telling him not to say anything. Sure, he found Cleo intriguing, but he didn't need the guys knowing that. They wouldn't get it. They were more into the busty blondes who wanted to have a good time. He wasn't in the mood to be taunted for his eye for the curvy, brunette, quiet type.

Justin nodded as if he got the message and leaned back in the booth, finishing the rest of his beer.

"So, it's cool then?" Nico looked at Kenny questioningly.

"What's cool?"

"If we have the party at our condo?"

"Yeah, sure. That's fine."

Kenny liked Mae. She came around a lot because she was Nico's sister, but she was nice and humble. She was normal, despite being married to the team's owner, Jonas. He was one of the wealthiest men in the city, but Mae didn't act like some trophy wife. Even though she was seriously pregnant, she still worked long hours at Pathletics, the athletic line she ran alongside Nate.

Kenny wondered if he would be at the party and took a big swig of his drink. He would deal with that when the time came. Even though he would see his long-lost brother in passing sometimes at games, they hadn't been stuck in the same room together since Kenny found out. It wasn't really a position he wanted to be in, but he couldn't avoid it, especially if the party was at his place.

"Cool. It won't be too big. I have pretty much everything planned. Chad hooked me up with a private bartender. Jonas gave me some suggestions for her favorite restaurants to cater. I just need someone to bake a cake or five. I swear Mae has triplets in there with how many sweets she's been eating," said Nico with a laugh.

"I don't even know why you're throwing her a party, anyway," said Kev, rolling his eyes.

"Uh, because she's my sister," Nico shot back.

"Still, it's not like she needs anything now that she's married to Jonas. She snatched him up real quick when he took over the company."

"Watch it, man," said Nico sharply, glaring at him.

"Settle down, boys," said Chad warily. "Kev, maybe you should just stop talking."

Kev leaned back in the booth and finished his beer with a sneer.

"I know a baker," said Kenny suddenly, something clicking in his head.

The team looked at him curiously.

"You do?" asked Nico.

"Sure!" Kenny looked to the bar and waved at Cleo. She looked up from drying glasses and raised a confused eyebrow.

Kenny didn't know what he was doing. The words were out of his mouth before he could stop them and his hand shot up involuntarily, but now it was out there. He wanted to help her, especially after what he witnessed at the café earlier in the day. He figured she could use a pick-me-up.

He watched as she set down a glass slowly and looked behind her nervously as if making sure he was waving to her. Kenny nodded assuredly and kept waving for her to come over. He watched as she wiped her hands on her apron and looked around the bar as if for help. She lifted the bar door and ducked underneath it before making her way to their booth.

Kenny turned to Nico. "See? A baker."

"Excuse me?" she asked, clearly confused.

"Nico was just saying how he needed someone to bake a cake for his sister's birthday party. I remembered last week how you mentioned you bake."

He avoided bringing up seeing her at the café because he didn't want her to feel embarrassed.

"I… uh… well, yes. I do bake, but I…" Cleo stammered. She clearly didn't like being on the spot.

"Can you make a red velvet?" Nico asked.

She swallowed nervously. "Yes. Yes, I can."

"What else can you bake? See, she's pregnant and is craving everything."

"Um, I do cookies, cake pops, French pastries, cupcakes. Really anything."

Nico nodded enthusiastically. "Perfect."

"Are you sure you want to hire *me*? Just right on the spot like this?" Kenny wished he could will her to have more confidence.

"That's okay. My boy, Kenny, here says you're a baker. That's good enough for me." Nico put his arm around Kenny and gave him a shake, as the rest of the team smiled knowingly at him. He realized he had sold himself out.

Cleo nodded nervously.

"What was your name again?" asked Nico, finally letting go of Kenny, who was squirming.

"Cleo." She smiled softly, and Kenny could see it was genuine, maybe even excited.

"Can you meet tomorrow to go over menu ideas?" asked Nico.

"Um, sure. I can do that."

"Come by the Trillium condos at 11 a.m. tomorrow. Just tell the doorman you're there to see Nico Klein."

"I'll be there." Cleo looked at Kenny quickly. Her eyes seemed to be dancing. She gave him a little nod as if to say thank you before walking away. He watched her for a moment before turning his attention back to the table, where his teammates' eyes were boring into him.

"Soooo…Cleo, huh?" asked Chad with a grin.

"What?" Kenny shrugged.

"*What* he says." Nico laughed.

"You've got a thing for the Pillsbury dough girl." Kev sneered.

Kenny swallowed hard. As much as he wanted to punch Kev in the face, he kept his cool. "She's a baker. You needed a baker," said Kenny nonchalantly.

"*Suuuure.*" Chad nodded sarcastically.

Kenny chugged the rest of his beer and waved at Bridget, who was dropping drinks at the table over.

"Can we get another round of beer and some tequila shots?" he asked as she sidled up to the table.

"Coming right up." She winked.

60

"I thought you were taking it easy tonight," asked Justin, giving him a curious look.

"I changed my mind."

He didn't want anyone asking him any more questions or making a big deal out of nothing. Because it was nothing. He was just helping out someone who needed it. Yes, she had brown doe eyes and a behind he wanted to dig his fingertips into, but he wasn't going to get involved. He just wanted someone fun for a night, not someone for life, and she was definitely someone for life. Just not his someone.

Bridget came by with a tray full of drinks and the team cheered. Kenny shot his tequila back and chased it with his beer.

"Thatta boy!" shouted Chad, following suit.

The rest of the night consisted of more drinks and, much to the liking of the team, a bachelorette party that walked in the doors.

"It's our lucky night, boys!" cheered Kev, as Bridget led the group of seven women to a nearby table.

While the rest of his teammates ogled over the bride-to-be and her friends, Kenny snuck in a glance at Cleo, who was busy writing something down behind the bar. She bit her lip as she concentrated. When she was finished, she tucked the pencil behind her ear and smiled to herself. Kenny couldn't help but wonder what she was thinking.

Squeals of laughter coming from the table next to them broke him from his thoughts. The bachelorette party was squeezing into their booth.

"I don't think there's enough room for us," one of them said, giggling.

"We'll make room," said Chad confidently. "Or you can just sit on our laps." He patted his thighs as one of the bachelorettes squeezed in and sidled up on his lap. The rest of them followed suit, except for the bride-to-be, who sat on the top of the booth.

A blonde in a hot pink dress put her arm around Kenny's neck. "Can I sit with you?" she asked with a confident smile.

Feeling like he had to prove himself to his team, he nodded and leaned back into the booth to allow her to sit.

"Drinks! We need drinks!" shouted Chad, pounding his fists playfully on the table. He looked around for Bridget, most likely, but frowned when he didn't see her. His eyes wandered to the bar where Cleo was handing a customer a drink.

"Cleo! We need you!" Chad waved at her.

Kenny felt himself sink a little into the booth. As much as he didn't want the team on his case about his little crush or whatever it was, he also didn't want Cleo to see this blonde on his lap.

"What can I get you?" Cleo asked as she walked up to the table, meeting everyone's eyes but Kenny's. He wondered if it was intentional.

"What do you ladies want?" asked Nico.

"Blow job shots!" the girls said in unison.

Cleo snorted under her breath. No one noticed but Kenny.

"Those will be right out." Cleo turned and avoided Kenny with her gaze.

Definitely intentional. He wondered for a moment if she was jealous, but laughed it off. She had no interest in him. She wasn't like the other girls.

At closing time, everyone paid their bills and began walking toward the door.

"Better go say goodbye to your *girlfriend*." Kev sneered at Kenny before nodding toward the bar. The rest of the team laughed cautiously.

Kenny put his arm around the blonde girl who nuzzled up to him. "Nah. I'm good."

Chapter 7

Cleo

Cleo's alarm clock blared loudly and she groaned, rolling over to turn it off. She slammed her hand on the button and lay her face down into her pillow. She desperately wanted to fall back asleep, but she knew she couldn't. No, she had to plan a menu of desserts for her biggest client ever. She groaned again.

Why had she agreed to this? She was an amateur. Clearly. The cafés didn't want her, and now some professional baseball player wanted her to cater his fancy party? This was ridiculous. She was playing pretend with the big shots. She felt her confidence dwindling as she lay in bed, exhausted from the night before.

She hadn't left the bar until after three a.m. The players had all stayed until close, which meant the rest of the patrons at the bar stayed late, too. After she was offered the catering job, her brain was being pulled in a million directions. It was a battle between cookie recipes and drink orders and willing herself not to look at that cute baseball player.

Why had he put her on the spot like that? Obviously, she was grateful for the opportunity, but he had barely spoken two words to her. When he had waved her over last night, she had felt an explosion of nervous butterflies that made her want to throw up. She had no idea what he wanted, and then he basically offered her a job. A small, stupid part of her thought maybe he was interested in her, but then she saw him leave with that pretty blonde girl.

As she closed up the bar, she was internally kicking herself for even thinking he saw her as anything more than someone who occasionally served him drinks. He probably referred her as a baker because he felt sorry for her after what he witnessed in the café.

She shut her eyes tight and shook her head into the pillow.

"You are an idiot," she whispered before pushing the covers off. She slowly climbed out of bed and headed to the kitchen, where she put on a large pot of coffee. She poured a steaming cup and sat at the kitchen counter with a notebook. For the next hour, she wrote down a few different menu options featuring her most-loved recipes. When she was satisfied with what she came up with, she went to get ready. She took a hot shower and wandered into her closet to pick an outfit. She picked out a pair of light-washed skinny jeans and a white linen button-down, and applied a little makeup, mostly sticking to the basics of concealer, mascara, and gloss. There wasn't time to dry her hair, so she pulled it into a low bun. Cleo shrugged at herself in the mirror. Good enough.

When she got in her car, she typed the name of the condos into her maps app. It was a twenty-minute drive. She was thankful for the drive ahead so she could calm her nerves with the windows down and some good music. She started feeling more herself until she pulled up the condo building. It was an all-glass high-rise with a large, flowing fountain in front and valet service. She pulled up slowly to the valet, who handed her a ticket and took her keys.

The confidence she was building on the way here had begun to slowly diminish. She looked down at her outfit and wondered if she should have dressed up more. She entered the large glass doors and walked toward the black marble front desk counter.

"Hello. May I help you?" asked the front desk man with a friendly smile.

"Um, yes. I'm here to see Nico Klein?"

"And what is your name?" he said as he pulled out a clipboard.

"Cleo. Cleo Aston." She realized she had never given her last name last night, and hoped her first name would be enough. She hadn't thought about the players and their need for security checks.

The man began running his finger down a list. He came to a stop and tapped the clipboard. "Here you are. I'll let him know you're here."

She nodded and watched him hit the *P* button on the desk phone.

"Mr. Klein. Your guest has arrived. Would you like me to send her up?" After a second, he nodded and hung up.

"He's expecting you. Take the elevators up to the penthouse floor. You'll need this key card for access." He handed her a slim white card.

"Thank you." She took it and smiled nervously.

Cleo let out a deep breath as soon as the elevator doors closed. She held the key card against the sensor and hit the *P* button. She watched as the floors grew higher and higher, and felt her nervousness grow with it. What was she *doing* here?

She should have expected him to live in a place like this. He was a professional athlete, after all. She just didn't expect to feel so out of place. When the elevator stopped, she put on a smile that she hoped was convincing and waited as the doors opened to an entryway that was bigger than her house.

She stepped out slowly and looked around. The floors were a dark wood which led to floor-to-ceiling windows straight ahead. She sucked in a breath at the view of the city. It was beautiful.

"Hello," a voice said.

Cleo looked and saw Kenny rounding the corner. He gave her a little wave. She felt her stomach drop all the way to the bottom floor of the building. What was he doing here? Her eyes wandered over him quickly. His hair was damp and he wore gray sweats with a matching hoodie. He was sexy without even trying.

"Um, hi," she stammered. "What are you doing here?" She immediately regretted asking.

"I live here," he said with a little laugh.

"Oh. Right. Sorry." She shook her head slightly.

"Nico's just finishing up a phone call." He rocked on his heels slightly.

Cleo nodded as an awkward silence fell over them. She looked down at her shoes. As if she wasn't nervous enough, now she had to be around one of the most handsome men she'd ever seen. There was no way she was going to get through this meeting if he was here. She felt eyes on her and willed herself to look up. Sure enough, he was looking at her, but looked away quickly. She couldn't read his expression. It was a mix between a smile and concern.

"There she is!" Nico called out as he walked into the room. "Thanks for coming."

Cleo nodded. "Thanks for having me. Your place is beautiful."

"Probably too beautiful for us." Nico laughed. "Can I get you anything to drink? Water? Coffee?"

"Coffee would be great," she said with a note of desperation.

"Yeah, I bet. Sorry we stayed so late." Nico waved for her to follow him down a short hallway and Kenny trailed behind. Soon they entered a kitchen that made her suck in a breath. It had white marble counters and a large butcher block island. The appliances were all top-of-the line and surrounded by towering white cabinets.

Composing herself, she said, "Oh, that's okay. I just hope you all had a great time."

"Too good. At least, I did. Kenny boy here ditched us and went home."

"I was tired." Kenny shrugged.

"That blonde was pretty disappointed," said Nico as he worked the coffee machine.

Cleo couldn't help but smile, and looked away so no one would see.

"Espresso okay?" asked Nico.

"Sure."

The smell of fresh coffee beans filled the kitchen as the espresso machine whirred. She had seen this kind of equipment in cafés, but never in someone's home. Nico handed her a glass mug, which she took thankfully before making their way to the living room. It was modernly furnished with professionally framed jerseys hanging on the walls. The three of them took a seat on the large, U-shaped couch in the center of the room. It was so plush she feared she might fall asleep on it.

She took a sip of espresso before getting to the reason why she was there.

"So, I put together a few menu ideas." She pulled her notebook from her purse and turned the pages. She wondered if she should have printed them out. Too late now.

"Sorry for the chicken scratch." She handed Nico the notebook.

He waved her off. "This is great."

He flipped through the pages as Kenny leaned over and read with him. She liked them. They were nice and weirdly normal for having more money than they probably knew what to do with. Kenny was certainly a surprise, but a pleasant one. She was glad it was these two, and not any of the other players. Some of them gave her the creeps.

"Uh-oh," said Nico suddenly.

"What?" asked Cleo worriedly.

"You have Kenny's weakness on here."

Cleo breathed a little sigh of relief and looked at Kenny curiously.

"Cowboy cookies." He smiled sentimentally, and Cleo felt lucky just to witness it. "My mom used to make them."

"Consider them on the menu." She smiled.

They spend the next thirty minutes finalizing the menu. They settle on a three-tiered red velvet cake with cream cheese icing, cowboy cookies, sea salt chocolate chip cookies, strawberry mini cupcakes, and lemon tiramisu bites. It was the largest order she'd ever done, but she was up for the challenge.

She finished up writing the details in her notebook before closing it shut. Nico leaned back on the couch and put his hands behind his head. He looked to Cleo and then to Kenny with a little smirk.

"So, you never did tell me how this came about."

Kenny shot Nico a look that Cleo pretended she didn't see. He seemed flustered, and she fought back a smile.

"Well, I saw her the other day at the café and remembered she was a baker. Just worked out, I guess."

Cleo was happy he didn't tell the whole story of her being rejected by the owner. She gave him a look that said *thank you*. He nodded and gave her a small smile.

"I've been baking for as long as I can remember, but am now just dipping my toes into the business side of it," said Cleo. "I hope to own my own bakery someday."

"That's really cool." Kenny nodded, and Cleo could tell he was being genuine.

Nico checked his watch. "We gotta head to practice, man." He stood from the couch and held out his hand. "Cleo, it's been a pleasure doing business with you."

She shook his hand. "Thank you for the opportunity."

He looked at Kenny and smiled mischievously.

"Kenny, can you walk her out? I have to get my stuff ready."

Nico walked off toward a long hallway. Cleo stood from the couch, gathering her things. She tried to calm her nerves, but being alone with Kenny made it almost impossible. He led her to the elevators and pressed the button. Suddenly, he turned to face her. She stopped in her tracks and looked up at him curiously.

"I should probably get your number. You know, for the party." He slid a hand through his hair and Cleo momentarily wished she was doing the same.

"Oh, sure." She recited her number and he typed it into his phone.

"I'll send it to Nico," he said as he slid his phone in his pocket.

She nodded as the elevator doors opened. She gave a little wave goodbye before sliding past him. It wasn't until the elevator doors closed behind her that she let out a breath she didn't know she was holding. She felt hopeful, for the first time in a long time. Was it because of the job or who she just left?

Chapter 8

Kenny

Kenny shoved his duffel bag in the overhead compartment and plopped down in the seat next to Nico. They were heading to an away game on the West Coast. As the rest of the team passed him in the aisle to find their seats, he nodded. Then he pulled his hat over his eyes and leaned his head back against the headrest. He just wanted to get some sleep after staying up late last night. Since Justin was leaving for New York today, they stayed up having a fcw beers on the patio. Kenny didn't fall asleep until around three a.m., and he thought he was being responsible by not going out to the bars with the rest of his team.

"You all right, man?" asked Nico as he flipped through the movies on the little TV set in the seat in front of him.

"Yeah. Just tired."

"We missed you last night. There were some beauties out at that new club that just opened."

"Next time." Kenny shrugged.

"Something tells me you're not really interested anyway."

Kenny lifted the cap of his hat and eyed Nico curiously. "What's that supposed to mean?"

"Come on, man. I saw the way you were looking at the baker girl."

"Cleo. And I was *not* looking at her."

"You weren't *not* looking at her." Nico smiled.

Kenny pulled his hat down again, shaking his head.

"Hey, she's cute. And for what it's worth, she was looking at you, too." Kenny felt Nico nudge him before he put his headphones on.

Kenny couldn't help but smile to himself. He thought he had caught her looking a few times, but he wasn't sure. Now there was a witness. He thought back on yesterday and the few moments alone he had with Cleo. She really was beautiful in a way where she didn't have to try, and she smelled like jasmine. Her perfume lingered after the elevator doors closed behind her and Nico spent a minute or two trying to place the scent.

Now he had her number, but it wasn't like he was going to do anything with it. Was he? He internally shook his head and reminded himself that it was just business. He didn't want to complicate anything. His life was simple. Baseball, and that was it. That's how he preferred it. After what happened with Sylvie, his trust when it came to women was almost nonexistent. It was better to not get too close.

He dozed after the plane took off and woke up when the wheels hit the runway.

"Rise and shine, sleeping beauty," said Nico, lifting the window shade. "Time to win this game."

The team rode the bus to the stadium, and everyone was trying to hype themselves up for the big game. It was one of their biggest rivals and the pressure was on. Kenny put on his headphones and listened to old-school rock, trying to drown out the rest of the team. When they arrived at the stadium, there were already fans lined up outside, booing them as they walked off the bus. Kenny just turned his music up louder. He was used to this.

Inside the locker room, they went over stats as they unpacked their equipment. Their coach was doing his best to get them motivated, but Kenny could feel the pressure. It was vibrating off the walls.

"I know this is a big game, but don't let that distract you. Just go out there and do your best," said their coach, inviting them into a huddle. They did their usual team chant before heading onto the field.

The game seemed to drag on. Every inning was a battle between the two teams. They kept up with each other's scoring, until the 11th inning when there was only one out remaining and Kenny struck out. The crowd went wild for their home team as Kenny threw his bat in anger and climbed down into the dugout. His teammates patted his back, but he waved them off. He was not in the mood for "it's okay" or "we'll get them next time."

The next few games away were no better for the team. They lost every single one, and while Kenny wasn't the one who struck out again, he still let it get to him. Since his life was baseball, he took everything to heart and his head. The other guys could brush it off better, but they had other things on their mind, like women and family. Two things Kenny didn't want to think about right now, especially knowing Nate would most likely be at Mae's party.

After their final away game ended in a loss, the team rode in silence back to the hotel. Kenny leaned his head against the window and watched the city lights pass by.

"All right, boys. I know it's been a rough week, but it's over now. Once we're back in Boston, we'll be back on top," said their coach, standing at the front of the bus. Seeing his little pep talk was falling on deaf ears, he sat back down, defeated.

Chad stood up suddenly. "Wake up, boys. We may not be going home with a win, but we can bring some ladies home tonight!"

The team whooped and threw their fists in the air.

"First bar we get to tonight, first round of drinks are on me!" yelled Chad.

The team let out another shout as the bus pulled up to the hotel. They all clambered out and headed through the lobby doors.

Back in his room, Kenny took a long, hot shower and put on his sweats before plopping down on the king-sized bed. He reached for the remote and clicked the TV on. He was scrolling through the guide when there was a knock on his door. He groaned and walked slowly over, looking through the peephole. It was Nico.

Kenny opened the door. "What's up?"

"We're heading out," said Nico, looking at Kenny's sweats.

"I'm staying in." Kenny shrugged.

"I thought you might say that." Chad pushed his way inside behind Nico, holding a bottle of tequila.

Kenny threw his head back, annoyed. Nico mouthed "sorry" as he trailed behind.

"You're not staying in. It's our last night here and we have some chaos to cause." Chad opened the bottle of tequila and took a swig before passing it to Kenny.

Kenny shook his head. "I'm good, man."

Chad plopped down on the bed and lay down, crossing his arms. "You know I'm not going to leave until you get dressed and come out." He smirked, taking another swig of tequila. "I can call the rest of the team in here." He rolled over to grab the hotel phone.

"Fiiiiine." Kenny rolled his eyes.

"Yes!" yelled Chad.

"Can you get your asses out of here so I can change?"

Chad gave him a little salute and stood up from the bed. He marched dramatically toward the door. "See you in the lobby in five." Nico followed behind him, smirking at Kenny.

Kenny shut the door behind them and got dressed in a pair of black jeans and a grey long-sleeved shirt. He headed downstairs and saw his team waiting outside the lobby doors. A party bus had just pulled up, with colorful lights flashing from inside. That had to be Chad's doing. Kenny let out a sigh and met his teammates outside.

The bus started the drive toward the city as they cracked open a few beers and music blasted through the speakers. They probably only drove for about fifteen minutes before reaching their first stop. It was a nightclub with a line wrapped around the building. The driver of the bus got off and talked to security briefly, who looked toward the bus curiously. He nodded and then waved to them. They clambered off the bus and he lifted the velvet rope, letting them pass. Everyone in the line groaned.

Inside, Chad stayed true to his word and bought everyone a round of shots. He was happy to order from the bartenders, who were all wearing bikinis and go-go boots. Kenny cheered his teammates before taking his shot. He didn't want to get too crazy tonight. He was still feeling defeated and tired. Instead, he'd keep an eye on his teammates and make sure no one got into too much trouble. If anything, they would keep him entertained.

He leaned against the bar and watched as a few of his teammates made their way onto the dance floor. Nico found a pretty brunette to dance with, and Chad had convinced one of the bartenders to leave her post. None of them really had any moves, but the girls didn't seem to care. Kev then walked out with gusto. He spotted a blonde girl at a high-top and asked her to dance, but she politely shook her head no. He didn't seem to get the hint because he grabbed her hand and tried pulling her onto the floor. She snatched her hand back and shook her head.

Kenny moved to step in. He knew Kev could be   a   creep. "Hey, man, I think she said no. Let's go get another drink." He patted Kev on the back and nodded toward the bar.

"Mind your business, man." Kev jerked away from him.

"But one of the bartenders was asking for you," Kenny lied.

Kev took a look at the bar and smiled before turning to walk away, but not before saying, "You're not that cute, anyway," to the girl.

She shook her head and let out a soft laugh as she watched Kev go. Kenny turned to follow, but she put her hand on his arm.

"Thank you," she said.

Kenny looked down at her. She was pretty and had a nice smile. Her eyes were a dark blue, and they were eyeing him eagerly. Her black dress left little to the imagination and his eyes couldn't help but wander momentarily.

"No problem." He flashed her a smile.

"Do you want to dance?" she asked, leaning in closely.

"What?" He could barely hear her over the music.

She leaned in closer, pressing her body against his and standing on her tiptoes so her face was close to his.

"Do you want to dance?" she asked again.

He knew this would be a one-night thing. She was hot. They were leaving tomorrow. Why not? But for some reason, looking down at this girl, he saw Cleo flash through his mind. She was in her pink sundress and high-tops. Effortlessly beautiful, and completely unaware of it. Kenny smiled at the thought of her.

"You know I'd love to, but I should really keep an eye on the rest of my team," said Kenny.

"Team? Are you an athlete?" asked the blonde.

Kenny nodded distractedly before turning to join Nico and Chad at the bar.

"Please tell me you're coming over here to buy that girl a drink," said Chad, eyeing the blonde.

"Sorry to disappoint." Kenny shrugged.

"Come on, man!" yelled Chad, exasperated. Kenny laughed and ordered one more beer before sneaking out and grabbing an Uber back to the hotel. He just wanted to watch a movie and doze off.

The rest of his teammates were hurting on the flight home the next day, and Kenny was glad he wasn't one of them. He was still tired, though. When he got back to his condo, he headed straight for the shower and then fell face down onto his bed. He was exhausted and was looking forward to a day off tomorrow to rest.

His phone vibrated and he unlocked it to see all the notifications he had been ignoring the past few days. He scrolled through the texts and missed calls quickly, almost missing a text from Cleo. He sat up quickly and opened it. She had sent a group text to him and Nico:

I have some samples ready to try!

Kenny lay back and placed his phone on his chest. He smiled to himself before dozing off.

Chapter 9

Cleo

Cleo moved around her kitchen quickly, pouring flour into one bowl and whisking frosting in another. The place was a mess, and so was her brain. She had been doing multiple batches of cupcakes, tweaking things with each bake to see which one was the winner. This party was a big deal and she wanted to get it right.

It also didn't help that she still hadn't heard back from Nico or Kenny. Maybe they had changed their minds and gone with someone else to cater the party. They would have at least told her, right?

She let out a sigh as she poured the batter into a pan. She popped it in the oven and set the timer before finally taking a little break. She leaned against the countertop and wiped her hands on her apron and looked around at the bowls and spoons cluttering the frosting-covered countertops. She was usually a neater baker than this. Clearly, she was stressed.

Her phone dinged and she looked around the kitchen frantically. Hopefully, it would be a reply and give her confirmation that all this wasn't for nothing. She searched the countertops for her phone, but came up empty-handed. She opened the drawers, but didn't find it, and searched cabinets with no luck. She heard another ding and looked curiously at the empty bag of flour sitting on the counter. Reaching inside, she found her phone.

"Nice one, Cleo," she said, shaking her head.

She unlocked her phone and saw a text notification. It was Kenny, and she'd be lying if her heart didn't skip a beat:

I can swing by to try the samples. I can head over in 30 minutes.

Cleo wasn't anticipating Kenny to come. She thought this was Nico's thing. She bit the inside of her cheek and read the text again. Why did she feel so nervous all of a sudden? She was already nervous before, but now it was multiplied by the fact this cute guy was going to come over. And be in her kitchen. And try her baking. And see her in this state.

She replied: *Sure. I'll text you the address.*

Cleo typed in her address and hit send before taking a deep breath. It was time to get to work. She pulled the cupcakes out of the oven to let them cool and then began frantically cleaning the kitchen. She basically threw everything in the sink and began scrubbing the dishes and arranging a few things in the dishwasher. She wiped off the counters, grabbed a broom, and swept the floor from sugar and flour. Then she arranged the desserts on different trays until she was happy with the presentation.

She looked around, satisfied with her work and then heard a knock at the front door. He was here. She walked toward the front door and saw her reflection in the entryway mirror.

"Oh, my God," she gasped.

There was frosting clinging to her hair and flour sprinkled across her forehead. She wiped away the flour and began trying to untangle the frosting that was dried like cement to her brown hair. There was another knock at the door. This was the best it was going to get. She took a deep breath and opened the door.

Kenny stood on the front step and gave her a smile. She smiled back as she took him in quickly with her eyes. He was wearing blue jeans and a white T-shirt that wasn't tight, but hugged his muscular arms in a non-trying way. He had a baseball cap on and his long hair peeked out from underneath. She was suddenly even more self-conscious.

"Hi," she said.

"Hi." He gave a little wave.

They looked at each other for a moment before Cleo caught her bearings.

"Come in, come in." She waved him in and stepped aside.

When he stepped past her, she could smell his aftershave and tried to hold on to the delicious scent. He looked around the living room as if taking everything in.

"This is a nice place," he said, looking toward the kitchen.

"Thanks." Cleo took his momentary distraction to look in the mirror again. She wiped some flour from her nose and tucked a piece of frosting-covered hair behind her ear. When she turned from the mirror, she saw Kenny smiling at her amused. She felt her cheeks burn.

"Sorry, I'm a mess." She looked down, embarrassed.

"Not at all." He gave her a reassuring smile.

She nodded before moving past him, leading him to the kitchen.

"The samples are just over here," she said, motioning to the countertop.

"You made all of these?" His eyes widened.

"Mhmm."

"These all look incredible. You must have been up all night." Kenny looked from the desserts to her, surprised.

"It's no biggie." She shrugged, even though she had been up until three a.m.

She watched as he looked at each of the trays. There were miniature versions of everything they had decided on for the menu, including the red velvet cake and cowboy cookies. She watched his gaze land on the cookies.

"Go ahead. Try one." She nodded encouragingly.

He carefully picked one up and took a bite. She watched as he closed his eyes and a smile spread across his face.

"These are even better than my mom's," he said with disbelief. "But don't tell her I said that."

She laughed, and then her eyes fell on the cupcakes sitting on the stovetop. She had forgotten to frost them in the frenzy of cleaning the kitchen.

"Oh, my gosh. I totally forgot to frost the strawberry cupcakes," she said, walking to the fridge and opening it to search for the frosting.

"No worries. I'm in no rush."

She smiled to herself as she pulled the bowl out and set it on the counter. She carefully popped out the cupcakes and set them on a plate, then opened a drawer and found a small spatula.

"Make yourself comfortable," she said, nodding toward the kitchen table.

"Actually, can I watch you work?" Kenny asked, nodding toward the cupcakes.

"Um, sure."

He nodded and leaned against the counter. His closeness made her breath pick up and she tried to keep her hands from shaking as she carefully frosted the cupcakes. She heard him inhale.

"It's fresh strawberries," she said knowingly.

"It smells amazing."

"Here. Try the frosting." She held the bowl up.

"Really?"

"Yeah, these are just samples, anyway. Dig in."

He dipped a finger in the frosting and put it in his mouth. She held her breath, waiting for a response. She watched as his eyes rolled back before closing. He let out a little groan. "Mmmmm."

Cleo felt a burning desire between her legs as involuntary thoughts entered her head before she quickly pushed them away. What was she thinking?

Kenny opened his eyes and looked at her with appreciation. "What did you *put* in that?"

She let out a little laugh, picking up the spatula again, and continued frosting the cupcakes. He continued watching her as she finished the last one. She set them carefully on a cupcake stand and stood back to admire her work.

"That's everything," she said. She untied the back of her apron and slid it up and over her neck. She hung it on a hook on the wall, and leaned against the counter next to Kenny. He looked at her and smiled.

"Here," he said as he reached his hand to her face.

She closed her eyes for a moment, wondering what he was doing, but not about to fight it. He took his thumb and gently wiped her cheek before pulling away. The hair on her neck stood up as her eyes fluttered open.

"You had a little flour there."

"Thanks." She fought back the smile that felt like it was going to explode onto her face.

"So how long have you been baking for?" he asked.

"Since I was little. My grandma taught me. Ever since I baked my first cake, I knew it was what I wanted to do with my life."

Kenny nodded. "That's how I was when I hit my first ball."

"And look at you now."

"And what about *you*? You've got to pursue this."

"I'm trying. It's not as easy as I thought." Cleo shrugged, thinking of the café.

"Don't let anyone make you doubt yourself," he said, as if reading her mind. "You're amazing. I've been to big catered events, and nothing's tasted this good." He nodded toward the trays of desserts.

"Thank you. Really. I needed that."

"No problem."

They sat in a comfortable silence for a minute. Cleo was surprised at how normal he was and how good she felt around him. She wondered what he was thinking. She peeked over at him, only to find him looking at her.

Flustered, she said, "I have some pastry boxes. I can pack this up for you. Maybe have Nico try them."

"Sure," he said. "That would be great."

She nodded as she pushed off the counter and opened a nearby cabinet. She pulled down a few boxes and began filling them. She stacked them on top of one another and handed them to Kenny.

"Thanks," he said, as he took the boxes carefully from her.

She led him toward the front door and opened it for him. He nodded appreciatively as he passed her. He stepped down from the front step before turning to her.

"Well, thank you for inviting me over and letting me try everything. These are going to be a hit." He looked down at the boxes in his hands before smiling up at her.

"Of course. Thanks for coming." She leaned against the doorway and watched him walk to his car. It was a jet-black sports car she knew nothing about, other than it probably cost more than her house. He gave her a little wave before sliding in and starting the ignition.

Cleo turned and closed the door behind her, leaning against it. She heard him pull away from the curb and let out the smile she had been stifling. Wow. All she could think was wow. Even though her stomach was basically doing backflips, she felt a wave of tiredness wash over her.

She trudged up the stairs to her bathroom and turned on the shower. As the steam filled the air, she stepped out of her jeans and slid off her T-shirt, tossing them on the floor. She opened the door to the shower and felt the hot water wash over her. Taking a deep breath, she slowly let it out. This was exactly what she needed.

She lathered soap onto her hands and glided them over her body, as the past hour with Kenny replayed in her head. She thought of his unruly hair trying to escape the hat on his head. The dimples that showed only when he smiled a certain way. How his jaw tensed when he was watching her. The smell of his aftershave, a mix of jasmine and neroli. The face he made when he tried her baking, and the groan he let escape from his throat.

She let her hands explore, as she replayed the animalistic sound in her head. Her hands trailed up her stomach and cupped her breasts before squeezing them as she looked up toward the water. The water dripped down, and her right hand followed. She pressed her palm against herself and rubbed in slow, circular motions as she imagined Kenny's hands against her, his mouth on her breasts. Her breath became shallower as she moved rhythmically, thinking of her body pressed against his, feeling his girth growing against her. Seeing his eyes roll back and the groan escape his lips, she let out a moan as she shuddered against her hand.

Chapter 10

Kenny

On the drive home, Kenny rode with the windows down and listened to some classic rock. He smiled as the wind whipped through the car and his favorite song came on. He was in a much better mood since coming home from their losing streak on the road. As much as he didn't want to admit it, he knew Cleo had something to do with it.

He looked over at the boxes of desserts in the passenger seat and smiled. The time he spent with her was surprisingly comfortable. She was warm and passionate about her dreams, and completely normal. Most of the women he met were eager to know him because of his job, not because of who he was as a person. Cleo didn't seem to care or ask any questions about his career, which was refreshing. She wasn't pretending to be anyone else.

He pulled into the underground parking of his condo, waving at the attendant as he passed. Once parked, he got out and whistled as he picked up the boxes to take upstairs. In the elevator, he thought about Cleo and her concentrated face as she worked in the kitchen.

It was attractive as hell to see a woman who was determined in what she did.

He then thought of him wiping the flour from her face. A pang of doubt hit him suddenly, as he wondered if he had overstepped. But he remembered her eyes gently closing, letting him touch her soft face for a moment. Did she feel something, too?

The elevator dinged as it reached the penthouse floor. The doors opened and he stepped into the entryway. He set his keys down and carried the boxes into the kitchen where Nico sat eating lunch.

"Hey, man," Kenny said casually.

"Hey. What's that?" Nico eyed the boxes curiously.

"Oh, they're samples from Cleo." Kenny set the boxes on the counter.

"Oh shoot. I forgot to text her back."

"No worries. I took care of it."

"I can see that." Nico gave him a smirk.

"I just figured we should get the ball rolling on this party. You know? Just want the best for Mae's birthday," said Kenny rushed.

"Riiiight. I didn't know you were *so* into party planning," said Nico sarcastically.

"Yeah, well, I didn't want to be rude and not respond, so I texted her back and tried the samples, and now we're all set. Just wanted to help out." Kenny was getting exasperated because he knew he was just digging himself a hole by talking more.

Nico let out a laugh before shaking his head and taking a bite of his sandwich.

"What?" asked Kenny with a shrug.

"Just admit it, man."

"Admit what?"

"That you have a thing for this girl."

"For Cleo?"

"Yes, Cleo."

"Nah. It's just business. You needed someone for the party, that's all."

Nico set his sandwich down and looked at Kenny, raising an eyebrow.

"It's okay to like someone, and for more than a one-night type thing."

Kenny looked down at his shoes. "I don't let myself. Not anymore."

The only person who knew about his past was Justin. He hadn't told anyone else about Sylvie, and how she had really messed him up. Maybe if Nico knew, he would understand and not push this so much. He had become a good friend, after all.

"I had someone back in college. We were high school sweethearts. I was going to propose. The whole thing. She cheated on me with someone almost twice her age. Her boss at her internship, who had a wife and a kid himself."

"Shit, Kenny. I had no idea." Nico shook his head in quiet disbelief.

"Yeah, well, since then I don't really want anything serious."

"I can understand that." Nico nodded.

"I'm hoping you can keep that to yourself."

"Of course, man."

Kenny nodded and started fixing himself a sandwich. Even after all of the desserts, he was hungry. He rummaged through the fridge and then laid everything out on the counter. Nico set his plate in the sink and made his way over to the dessert boxes. He opened each one and inhaled deeply.

Kenny smiled. "Wait until you try them."

Nico reached in and pulled out a mini red velvet cake. He took a bite and suddenly held it out in front of him, as if inspecting it.

"What sort of voodoo is this?" he asked, his eyes widening.

Kenny laughed. "Told you."

He watched as Nico tried each dessert one by one in silent appreciation. Kenny felt something bubbling up inside of him. It was a small feeling of pride for Cleo, which was unusual. He tried to ignore it and continued making his sandwich.

Nico leaned against the counter, shaking his head.

"Get these away from me," he said, pushing the boxes away.

Kenny laughed.

"You were right about her. She's good. Really good."

"Mae is going to be one happy pregnant woman."

"And *you* could be one happy man if she was feeding you this on the regular."

Kenny rolled his eyes.

"No wonder she's a little, you know, plump. I didn't know you had a thing for the curvy ones."

Kenny held up the butter knife he was spreading mayo with and pointed it non-threateningly at Nico. "I don't have a thing for her. And don't make fun of her size."

Nico held his hands up and slowly backed away, letting out a little laugh.

"By the way, some of us are going out tonight. Nothing too crazy."

"Yeah, maybe."

Nico walked out of the kitchen and headed to his bedroom. Kenny sat at the counter and started eating his lunch. Maybe it would be good for him to go out tonight. Finding a girl for the night would get Nico off his case about Cleo. It would also be a good distraction for him because all he'd been thinking about since he'd left her house was Cleo.

He thought of her hair pulled back in a messy bun, with frosting stuck in it. The way she tried to fix herself up in the mirror without him knowing. The jeans and T-shirt she wore underneath her apron that showed she didn't try too hard and didn't have to. The satisfied smile she had when he tried her desserts.

He let out a sigh. This wasn't good. He finished his lunch and washed the dishes before heading to his room. He put on a movie and dozed off halfway through. A knock at the door hours later woke him up.

"Yeah?" Kenny called out.

"I'm heading out to meet some of the team for dinner and drinks. Are you coming?" asked Nico as he opened the door, peeking his head in.

"Nah. I think I'm going to stay in tonight."

"Booo."

Kenny waved him off. "Have fun."

Nico shut the door behind him. Kenny heard him grab his keys and the elevator doors ding. He sat up and rubbed his eyes. He checked the time. It was 7 o'clock. He had slept for a long time. He rolled off the bed and went into the bathroom to take a shower to wake himself up. Afterward, he pulled on some sweats and grabbed a cupcake from the kitchen. He devoured it in one bite.

He walked to the living room and plopped down on the couch. He looked around, wondering what to do. It had been a while since he had stayed in and had the place to himself.

He pulled his phone from his pocket and dialed his mom. They hadn't caught up in a bit.

The phone rang two times before he heard her pick up on the other line.

"Kenny! Hi!" she answered warmly.

"Hi, Mom. How are you?"

"I'm good. Just popped dinner in the oven. I'm so happy you called. I caught the games on TV. How are you?"

"Ah, yeah. That was some losing streak, huh?"

"You win some, you lose some. You boys will do better next time."

Kenny smiled. His mom was always encouraging.

"What are you doing, honey? You're usually out with the boys."

"Yeah, I thought I'd just stay in tonight."

"Mmm. Everything okay?"

"Yeah, Mom. Everything's fine."

He heard her setting the timer on the oven. Even though she lived alone, she still made an effort to cook for herself. She was an amazing cook. Maybe that's why he liked Cleo so much. She kind of reminded her of his mom, in all the best ways.

Kenny realized he hadn't visited his mom in a while and felt a pang of guilt. They would usually just meet in the city for lunch, but he should put in more of an effort. He knew she got lonely sometimes in her house. She had married a nice man years after Kenny was born. John was his name. Despite everything, he took in Kenny as his own and eventually adopted him. He died a few years back from a heart attack, which was devastating for his mom.

"Hey, Mom."

"Yeah, honey?"

"I want to come visit next week. We'll be playing home games all week, so I'll be in the city. I can come over for dinner or something."

"Oh, that would be great! I would love that."

She was silent for a moment.

"What's really going on, honey?" she asked curiously.

"What do you mean?"

"I don't know. You sound... different."

"Do I?"

"Oh, my gosh. Is it a girl?"

Kenny rolled his eyes. His mom was always pushing him to get out there and meet a girl. She was just waiting for the day he would bring someone home to meet her. She'd always say, "I need grandbabies, you know. You're my only hope."

This time, he didn't want to disappoint her with his usual answer. This time, he actually felt like there could be, and who else better to admit it to than his mom?

"No. Maybe. I don't know," he said exasperatedly, running a hand through his damp hair.

He heard his mom squeal on the line and he had to pull his phone away from his ear.

"Really? Oh, my gosh. What's her name? When do I get to meet her?"

"Slow down, Mom. Her name is Cleo. And I don't know if you'll ever meet her. It's new. It's not even anything."

"Not yet! Tell me about her."

"She's a baker. A really good one. She's quiet, but nice. I don't know. She's different."

"Smart girl. She knows a way to a man's heart is through his stomach. That's how I got John," she said, her voice breaking a little.

"You okay, Mom?"

"Yeah, yeah. I'm fine. Sorry. So, have you asked her out?"

"No. I don't know if I'm going to."

He heard his mom let out a sigh.

"Honey, you can't be afraid forever. I know what happened with Sylvie was…"

"Please don't."

"All right, all right. I'm just saying. It's been a long time since you've gotten back out there. And you know I need grandbabies."

Kenny smiled. "I know. I'm your only hope."

"Exactly. Ask this Cleo girl out."

"Yeah, maybe."

They talked for a little while longer about his upcoming schedule and about the charity event she was putting on at the local school. They set up a night for the next week for him to come visit her. She only lived an hour away, so it wasn't difficult for him to get away. They said their goodbyes, and Kenny clicked his phone off. He smiled. He always felt happier after talking to his mom.

He thought about what she said about asking Cleo out, but he wasn't ready. He didn't tell her that because he didn't want to disappoint her. Maybe he shouldn't have said anything at all, but it was nice to talk about her after the time they'd shared. He sighed. If anything, they could just be friends.

Chapter 11

Cleo

Cleo finished putting away the dishes on the counter. The kitchen was finally back to normal after yesterday. She stacked her mixing bowls in the cabinet and placed the last cupcake tray in the pantry. She breathed a sigh of relief as she took a look around. Thankfully, she would have a few days off from baking. As much as she loved it, all this prep for the party was tiring.

She glanced at the counter where Kenny had been standing yesterday and smiled to herself. It didn't feel real that he had even been here at all, but he had been. He had watched her do what she loved and seemed to enjoy it. He had wiped flour from her cheek, leaving goosebumps on the back of her neck. It was one of the best afternoons she'd had in a while.

Now it was back to real life. She was working at the bar tonight, and checked her phone for the time. She had a few hours until she needed to be there. A notification popped up just then. It was Kenny. She smiled and opened the text:

Nico loved everything. There's almost nothing left. Practice is going to be rough.

After walking to the living room, she collapsed on the couch with a sigh. She read his text again and couldn't help but feel giddy. She felt embarrassed feeling that way, like a schoolgirl or something. She couldn't help it, though. There was something about Kenny that made her nervous in the best way, and excited. Clearly. She thought about the steamy shower after he left, and blushed.

She hadn't done that in a while, and even when she had, it had never felt that good or real. She almost felt guilty about thinking of him in that way. Almost. She was sure a lot of girls swooned over him. He was a good-looking professional baseball player. She glanced at his text again. How many other girls was he texting? She knew this was just business, but still felt excited to text him back:

Glad to hear it. Have a good practice. ☺

She wondered if the smiley face was too much. Too late now. She set her phone on the coffee table and flipped on the TV to relax a little before work. She found a rom com and lay back, pulling a chunky knit blanket over her.

Two hours later, she woke with a start. The movie credits rolled as she grabbed her phone to check the time. She had to be at work in half an hour. She ran upstairs and rummaged through her closet for her favorite pair of jeans, slid them on, and grabbed one of her Murphy's T-shirts.

In the bathroom, she brushed her hair out before putting it into a high ponytail. She applied a little lip gloss and gave herself a once over in the mirror. This was as good as it was going to get. She thought about the chance of seeing Kenny tonight, but didn't have time to put in any more effort. Besides, after yesterday's appearance, she could only go up from there.

Parking her car behind the bar, she headed in through the back door, and through the kitchen. She grabbed an apron and slid it over her neck while walking to the bar. It was slow, maybe only a few regulars who came after work, which wasn't surprising for a weeknight.

"Hey, Cleo." Bridget walked toward her, smiling warmly.

"Hey, Bridget. How has it been here the past few days?"

"Pretty slow. Not a lot to celebrate after the team's losing streak last week."

Cleo nodded as if she knew anything about the team and its stats. She couldn't help but feel sad for Kenny. Baseball seemed to mean a great deal to him, so losing must be hard.

"Bummer."

Bridget nodded. "It should pick up this weekend, though, since they'll be playing at home. I'm sure they'll be in to celebrate or drown their sorrows, which is always good for business."

Cleo smiled at the idea of seeing Kenny. "Definitely. So what would you like me to do while we wait for it to pick up?"

"A new shipment came in today. I've unloaded most of it, but I need to get the bottles on the shelves." Bridget nodded toward the kitchen.

"You've got it."

For the next hour, Cleo restocked the shelves in the back and front of the bar. When she was finished, business seemed to be picking up a little. She smiled warmly at the regulars and poured them their usual drinks. It was just her and Bridget tonight because one of the other bartenders had called out sick. They probably didn't need her, anyway. It looked to be a slow night.

"Did you catch that game the other night?"

Cleo's ears perked up a little while listening to two elderly regulars talk over their beers.

"It was like watching a bunch of amateurs," one of the men said, shaking his head.

"They need to get their heads in the game if they want to go all the way."

"They always get so close, and then blow it."

"That Michaels has some arm, though. The team could learn from him."

Cleo realized she didn't even know Kenny's last name. Checking to see that no one needed her, she slid her phone from her back pocket and searched the team's roster. She scrolled down and saw Kenny's face. He had a serious smile, and he looked sexy as hell in his uniform. She smiled when she saw that his last name was Michaels, and that the two men had been talking about him.

She heard someone clear their throat and looked up guiltily to see someone new had sat at the bar. She clicked off her phone and slid it in her back pocket.

"Sorry. What can I get you?" she asked.

"Whiskey. On the rocks."

She nodded and grabbed a glass, filling it with ice. The man looked familiar. He was young and she knew he had been in before, but couldn't place him. She filled the glass generously, hoping it would make up for her being on her phone.

"Here you go." She slid the drink across the counter.

"Thanks." He took a large sip and set his glass down, eyeing her.

She nodded and turned to busy herself with unloading the clean glasses from the washer. She could still feel his eyes on her, which she was pretty used to being a bartender, but she couldn't help but feel uncomfortable.

She glanced his way uneasily. "Is there something else you need?"

"No. Just looking." He shook his head casually.

She studied him for a minute before finally placing him. He was on the team and had always given her creep vibes. She wondered where the rest of them were, and wished it was Kenny sitting here and not him.

"You're on the team, right?" she asked casually.

"Yep. Kev." He took another sip of his drink.

"Just you tonight?"

"Yep."

"Well, let me know if you need anything else."

Cleo felt a little disappointed as she turned her back and began stacking glasses.

"I'm just enjoying the view, sweetheart."

She shook her head, hoping he didn't catch her.

"You ever been with a ball player before?" he continued.

"Can't say I have." She turned and shrugged.

"Well, I can change that."

Cleo pretended she didn't hear him and looked around to see if anyone needed her. She was on her own. Kev leaned in and smiled at her.

"What do you say about me taking you out tonight?"

"I'm working." Cleo looked around the bar as if it was obvious.

"After."

"I'm closing tonight."

"You're making this harder than it has to be."

"Nothing will be open at 3 a.m."

"My condo will be." He smirked at her, leaning back on the barstool.

"I don't think so."

He gave her an icy look and finished his drink. "I'll take another one."

Cleo turned to pull the bottle of whiskey from the shelf, rolling his eyes that he was staying longer. She poured him a less generous serving this time and slid his drink toward him.

Thankfully, the two elderly men who were chatting about the team earlier waved her over to order another round of beer. She poured their beer into frosted glasses and slid their drinks toward them with a thankful smile.

"That boy bothering ya?" one of them asked, nodding toward Kev.

"Oh no. It's fine. He comes on a little strong, but I think he's harmless."

"You let us know if he's causing you any trouble. He may be on the team, but that doesn't mean he's untouchable."

She nodded gratefully before getting back to placing glasses on the shelves. She heard Kev place his glass down loudly on the counter, as if trying to get her attention. Was he done already? If so, he was probably getting dangerously close to crossing the line more than he already had. She heard him clear his throat.

She turned around and raised a questioning eyebrow at his empty glass.

"Maybe you'd like some water? Or something from the kitchen?"

"I'd like another drink," he slurred.

Cleo looked around for Bridget, but she must have been in the back.

"Can you give me a second? I have another table that's waiting on me," she lied.

"You're playing hard to get." He placed his hands on the counter and leaned over it, his face close to hers. Cleo swallowed hard, but stood her ground even as his whiskey breath poured over her.

"I can wear you down," he whispered.

"I really have to get to my table."

Bridget walked through the kitchen doors and watched the uncomfortable exchange before marching over with authority. Kev spotted her and sneered at Cleo before putting a wad of cash on the bar. "I'll be leaving to find another bar with better service and hotter bartenders."

Bridget and Cleo watched him walk unsteadily toward the door. Cleo let out a sigh of relief when the door shut behind him.

"Are you okay?" asked Bridget, putting her hand on Cleo's back.

"I'm fine."

"You didn't look fine."

"He was just a little pushy."

"That guy is bad news, Bridget," one of the men said, shaking his head.

"I don't usually see him in here by himself. He's usually with the team," she said thoughtfully.

"Well, he's gone now," said Cleo, not wanting to make a big deal of it. She smiled at a group of customers who had just walked in. Bridget walked over to greet them, leaving Cleo to catch her breath after that threatening exchange.

She wondered if Kenny knew how much of a creep his teammate was. They seemed to be together a lot, which was strange because Kenny was such a nice guy. Kev didn't seem to be someone he would likely be friends with. Maybe it was just because they were on the same team. She started to dread the possibility of them coming in this weekend. As much as she wanted to see Kenny, the thought of Kev being anywhere near her creeped her out.

Maybe he had gotten the hint. If not, at least Bridget would look out for her, and a few of the regulars here. They were like a family and Cleo was thankful for them. She felt her phone vibrate in her back pocket. She pulled it out and glanced quickly at the notification lighting up the screen. It was Kenny. Surprised, she opened the text:

I thought you'd like to know I survived practice. ☺

She smiled down at her phone. Maybe this wasn't just business. She typed a quick reply:

I'm so glad to hear you made it through!

Maybe the smiley face wasn't too much after all.

Chapter 12

Kenny

Kenny ran into the locker room and threw his gear in his locker quickly before heading to the showers. He wanted to beat the rest of the team and get in a hot shower before they rushed in. He washed off the sweat and the red dirt from the long practice. As he shut the water off, he heard the rest of the team walking in. He grabbed a towel and dried off before wrapping it around his waist and walking over to his locker.

"Got some place to be?" asked Chad, looking amused as he threw his gear down.

"Yeah, you rushed off the field," said Nico, sitting on the bench and taking off his shoes.

"Just ready to get home," said Kenny as he rummaged through his duffel bag for clean clothes.

"What? You're not coming out for happy hour?" asked Chad disappointedly.

"Neither of us are," said Nico.

"Wait, what?" Chad looked between the two of them.

"We have to finalize a few things for Mae's party," said Nico.

"With the baker girl?" asked Chad, wiggling his eyebrows at Kenny.

Kenny ignored him and slid on a pair of sweats and pulled on his team hoodie.

"Yeah. She's bringing over the final menu to try out. She's really good. Wait until you try it." Nico headed toward the showers.

"I'm sure she is. Have you tried any of her goods, Kenny?" Chad smirked.

Kenny rolled his eyes.

"Wait, are you talking about that bartender girl?" asked Kev, joining the conversation.

"Yeah, why?" asked Kenny, eyeing him uncertainly.

"She seems like a real bitch."

"Excuse me?" Kenny could feel himself getting defensive, but tried to swallow his irritation down.

"Yeah, the other night I went into the bar and had a drink. Or two."

"And?"

"She just seemed like a snob."

"So she turned you down?" Chad laughed.

"She wishes. As if a professional ball player would want a fat service worker," Kev muttered, as he grabbed a towel and headed for the showers.

"Watch it." Kenny stepped in front of him and squared up. Kev looked startled for a moment before letting out a laugh and pushing past Kenny.

Kenny watched him for a moment angrily. Questions ran through his head. Had Kev come on to her? Why had he gone to the bar without the team? Was it to see her? He couldn't help but feel a little jealous, but remembered that she had most likely turned him down, based on Kev's attitude. Kenny smiled to himself. He was happy someone had put the creep in his place.

He grabbed his phone from the shelf in his locker and unlocked it. There was a text from Cleo. He opened it eagerly:

5 at your place?

He fought back a smile before he responded.

Yes. See you soon!

He locked his phone before sliding it in his pocket.

"Who was *that?*" Nico nudged him.

"Oh, it was Cleo. She'll be over at five with the final lineup of desserts for the party."

"Awesome. Thanks for setting that up. I'll see you back home."

Nico grabbed a towel and headed for the showers. Kenny strapped his duffel bag over his shoulder and said a few goodbyes to his teammates before heading to the parking garage. Nico didn't know that Cleo and he had been texting quite a bit outside of just party planning. He didn't want to make a big deal out of it because it *wasn't* a big deal. They were just friends.

They would text throughout the day. Not about anything personal, but just about day-to-day life. He enjoyed hearing about her baking or her funny stories from the bar. She cheered him up if there was an off-day at practice or pressure from the upcoming games. It was nice. Even though they had been texting, he still felt nervous to see her tonight. He hadn't seen her since that afternoon at her house.

Once Kenny got home, he started tidying up the condo. She was going to be over in an hour and he didn't want to come off as a slob, which he really wasn't. He just wanted it to look extra nice for her arrival. He wiped the kitchen counters and straightened the pillows on the couch. He was rummaging through the kitchen cabinets for glass cleaner when Nico cleared his throat behind him, startling him.

"Whatchya looking for?"

Kenny whipped around. "Oh, uh. Glass cleaner."

"Why?"

"I just wanted to wipe down the coffee table really fast."

"Mhmm." Nico smirked. "This wouldn't have anything to do with Cleo coming over, would it?"

Kenny threw a rag at him and turned back toward the cabinet. He found the glass cleaner and headed to the living room, snagging the rag from Nico. Once the place looked good, he sat on the couch and anxiously checked his phone for the time. She would be here any minute.

Just then, the elevator doors dinged and slid open. Kenny got up from the couch quickly, too quickly, and walked to greet Cleo who was balancing a stack of pastry boxes.

"Here, let me help you." Kenny grabbed the boxes and saw her smiling face appear.

"Thanks."

He moved the boxes awkwardly and cradled them with one arm, as he put his other arm around her in a quick hug. Her hair was damp and smelled like coconut. He wanted to get lost in it, but pulled back suddenly when he heard Nico walk up behind him. Nico gave him a knowing smile as he stepped quickly and reluctantly away from Cleo.

"Hey, Cleo. Thanks for coming." He waved her toward the kitchen.

"Of course. Are you getting excited for your sister's party?" Cleo set her purse on the entryway table and followed Kenny and Nico.

"Yeah. It's turning out to be bigger than I expected."

"Oh, wow."

"Yeah, I might have to order a few dozen more desserts. I hope that's okay."

"Yeah, I'm sure I can manage it. No problem."

Kenny set the pastry boxes carefully on the kitchen counter. He peeked inside one of the boxes and shook his head in amazement. The miniature cupcakes looked identical and they smelled decadent.

"These look amazing, Cleo."

"Go on. Open the rest up." She smiled at him. He could sense she felt proud, and it made him feel warm inside to see that confidence in her.

Kenny carefully opened each box while Cleo took a seat at the kitchen counter. Nico grabbed a few plates from the cabinet.

"You know what would go great with these?"

Kenny and Cleo looked at him questioningly.

"Some wine. What do you say, Cleo? Can you stay for a glass?"

Kenny continued unboxing the pastries, but glanced at her from the side of his eye. He watched as a nervous look came over her. He so badly wanted her to say yes.

"Uh, sure. That would be great." She looked down at her hands and Kenny watched a small smile form on her lips. He shot Nico a bemused look.

"You're welcome," mouthed Nico.

"Red or white?" asked Nico, as he opened up the wine fridge.

"Red would probably go best with the chocolate."

"You've got it." Nico grabbed a bottle and uncorked it expertly before pouring three glasses.

Kenny plated the miniature desserts and set them on the bar top before taking a seat next to Cleo. Nico sat next to him and handed them their wine. They clinked their glasses and each took a sip. Nico and Kenny began taking bites of each of the desserts. They *ooh*ed and *ahh*ed over every single one, before finally sitting back in their chairs.

Nico patted his stomach, while Kenny shook his head. Cleo watched them, amused.

"You're like the jedi master of cake," said Nico, wiping his mouth from crumbs.

Cleo let out a laugh and Kenny absorbed it. It was a genuine belly laugh, and he loved it.

"Seriously. Mae is not going to know what hit her." Kenny agreed.

"So, we can finalize the menu?" Cleo pulled a notebook from her purse.

"Yes to everything here, and add a dozen of each," said Nico.

She jotted down a few notes before closing her notebook. She took a sip of wine and emptied her glass. Kenny wondered if she would leave now that they were done, but he hoped she wouldn't.

"Would you like me to pour you another glass?" he asked.

Cleo looked at him curiously for a moment. He held his breath as he waited for her answer.

"Sure," she said, as she tucked a strand of hair behind her ear.

"Now that we have business out of the way, why not?" Nico slid his glass toward Kenny, who was carefully pouring wine.

For the next few hours, they sat in the kitchen sipping wine and talking about anything and everything. Kenny and Nico talked about the team and what went on behind the scenes. The truth was, they were all just a bunch of kids who somehow made it to the big leagues.

"You wouldn't think we were professionals at all if you saw what went down in the locker room," said Kenny.

"Seriously. With the pranks we pull, you'd think we were back in grade school." Nico smiled mischievously. "Do you remember the fish in Kev's bag?"

"The locker room smelled for weeks!" Kenny laughed.

Cleo laughed right along with them. She seemed like she was genuinely enjoying their stories, and Kenny was genuinely enjoying sitting so close to her.

"Wait. Kev… is he the—"

"Creep? Yeah, that's him."

Cleo bit back a laugh.

"I heard he came in the other night," said Kenny curiously. He wanted to know what had happened.

"Yeah. He did." Cleo took a sip of her wine.

He waited for her to continue.

"Uh-oh. What happened?" asked Nico, eyeing her.

"He was just a little pushy. He wanted me to go home with him," said Cleo quietly.

Kenny could feel heat rise to his face.

"Obviously, I said no," she said quickly.

"Yeah, he was all butt-hurt about it today." Nico laughed.

"Maybe he needs another fish in his bag," suggested Cleo.

Kenny smiled at that. The way she said it was so innocent. He hated that Kev had been such a creep to her. "I can arrange that," he said.

"You guys remind me of my brothers back home in Indiana. They're always up to something, I swear." She smiled down at her wine before taking a sip.

She told them more about her family and how she grew up with two older brothers who were always messing with her. Nico and Kenny laughed at her horror stories. Kenny couldn't remember the last time he had felt this comfortable with a girl, let alone in front of his friends. Nico seemed to like her too. He kept giving him looks like he was impressed. Cleo really fit in with them.

This was turning out to be too perfect. He knew what that meant. It meant it was either too good to be true, or it would blow up in his face. This thing, whatever it was, had to end. He picked up his glass and emptied it in one big gup before putting it back on the counter with a loud clink.

"Well, this was fun," he said, standing up and sliding his phone out of his pocket.

"Yeah…you going somewhere?" Nico raised an eyebrow.

"Yeah, I think I'm going to go meet the guys. They're going to that new bar that just opened. We're finished here, aren't we?" He looked at Cleo with a bored expression.

He watched as she shifted uncomfortably in her seat.

"Um, yeah. We're all set here," she said quietly.

"All right. Well, I'm off. Nico can walk you out."

Kenny turned and walked out of the kitchen, but not before seeing the hurt expression on Cleo's face. It crushed him and it took everything in him to not turn back around and stay. But staying meant someone would get hurt, and he couldn't risk it being him.

Chapter 13

Cleo

Cleo sat at the kitchen counter with her mouth slightly open as she watched Kenny walk out of the room without looking back. She listened to him grab his keys and walk into the elevator as the doors opened. Soon, it was silent. He was gone. Really gone. She sat there awkwardly with Nico and a wineglass in her hand. She took a breath in and set her glass on the counter, the clink the only sound between them.

What had just happened? She thought the night was going well. It was fun. She really felt like there might be something between them, even though this wasn't a date. How did he flip a switch like that? A look had washed over his face that made him unreadable. Unrecognizable. It was as if a storm had suddenly passed through him, and then he was gone. She furrowed her brow as these thoughts whirled around in her head.

Finally, she looked to Nico, who was witness to everything, and sat awkwardly two barstools down. She raised her eyebrows questioningly and hoped he would give her some answers.

"I don't know what that was," said Nico, clearing his throat and looking toward the front door. She believed him.

"Did I do something?" asked Cleo.

"Nah." Nico waved her off. "He was probably just in a bad mood or something."

Yeah right, she thought.

She straightened up in her seat and tucked her hair behind her ears, trying to calm the feelings that were flooding her. She had to get out of there. This was embarrassing and hurtful, and she didn't want Nico to see her looking upset. The last thing she needed was him telling Kenny she had gotten worked up. They'd probably laugh about it. Aww, the baker girl had a crush.

"Well, I should probably be going," she said calmly, even though her insides were stirring.

"Are you sure? I'm sorry about that."

"Yeah, I have to get home."

Yeah, okay. I'll walk you out." He rose from his barstool. She could tell he felt bad about his friend, but didn't know what to do since he was left to fend for himself.

Cleo took one look at where Kenny had been sitting and a replay of the night whizzed by in her head. His laughter. His arm brushing against hers. His looks he didn't know she caught. All tainted by his sudden and unexplained departure. She let out a small sigh as she followed Nico out to the living room.

"Don't worry about Kenny. I'm sure something just came up," said Nico, as if reading her thoughts. He pressed the button for the elevator and leaned against the wall, looking at his feet.

Cleo knew he was trying to be nice and spare her feelings. She gave him a small smile and walked through the elevator doors as they slid open.

"Thanks, Nico. I'm glad we were able to finalize the menu. If there's anything else you need, just let me know."

He gave her a little wave before the elevator doors shut. Now she could let her emotions out. She backed up slowly until her back reached the wall of the elevator. She leaned against the railing and looked up, trying to blink back tears. Which was it? A bad mood or a sudden engagement? Or was it that he simply lost interest in her? Or was he meeting someone? Another girl?

She looked at herself in the mirrored wall of the elevator and laughed quietly to herself. Who did she think she was? She looked at the yellow sundress she had put on and the curls that hung loosely by her face. She had actually tried using a curling iron because she wanted to look good for him. Now she felt like a fool. A tear rolled down her cheek and she wiped it away gruffly, just as she reached the floor of the parking garage.

She got in her car and pulled her hair into a messy bun, as if that would make her feel like her normal self. The one who didn't try, especially not for a guy. She turned the key in the ignition and was about to put it in drive, but she stopped. She didn't want to go home. She didn't want to be alone. She rummaged in her purse for her cellphone. It was just after nine. She didn't realize she had spent so much time there. It was kind of late, but she texted Elle anyway:

Can I come over?

Elle: *Of course. Is everything okay?*

Cleo: *Thanks. Be there soon.*

Cleo tossed her phone on her seat and began driving to Elle's apartment. In just ten minutes, she arrived. She found a parking spot and put change into the parking meter, then walked up to the door and pressed the button for Elle's apartment.

"Hello?"

"It's me. Can you buzz me in?"

She heard the loud buzz and the door click. She pushed it open and walked the two flights of stairs. Elle was waiting at the end of the hallway. She gave her a little wave and looked at her questioningly as Cleo walked toward her.

"Hi. Thanks," said Cleo, out of breath, giving her a quick hug.

"Of course. You didn't answer my question, though. Is everything okay?"

"Yeah, everything is fine." Cleo sighed.

Elle looked at her skeptically as she held open her apartment door. Cleo slid past her and walked to the living room where the TV was playing a murder documentary.

"You're obsessed." Cleo shook her head with a smile.

"This one is so good. Get this. The wife was innocent all along. It was actually their dog walker. I knew it. I called it in the first ten minutes. I'm telling you, I chose the wrong job. The Boston Police Department could really use me."

Cleo laughed. She already felt a little better.

"Sorry," said Elle sheepishly. She switched off the TV and sat next to Cleo. "What's up, Cleo?"

Cleo tilted her head back and rested it on the couch. "I don't know. There's this guy…"

"Wait. A guy? What guy?" asked Elle excitedly.

"Whoa, whoa. Calm down." Cleo looked at her and put her hands up.

Elle took a deep breath. "Okay. I'm calm."

"It's nothing, really. I was talking to this guy and I saw him tonight, but he made it clear he wasn't interested."

"This sounds like it calls for wine or ice cream."

"Ice cream."

"On it." Elle stood and walked to the kitchen, bringing back a pint of cookie dough and a pint of mint chocolate chip, and two spoons. Cleo grabbed the cookie dough and dug her spoon in, taking a bite.

"Thanks." She smiled at Elle appreciatively.

"So, who is this guy?"

"His name is Kenny. He's a baseball player."

"I knew you'd finally take my advice and talk to one of them. You couldn't resist the tight pants, huh?" Elle pointed a spoon at her excitedly.

"He's different. He's a quiet type, until he opens up, which I thought he was doing. Oh, and Elle, he's so cute. Like *so* cute."

"This is so exciting, Cleo."

"Yeah, but tonight he just shut off."

"Walk me through it."

Cleo spent the next few minutes telling Elle everything about being hired for the party, and the non-business text messages, and the fun night she had with him.

"Hmm." Elle looked thoughtful for a moment. "I don't hear anything that would have made him leave like that."

"I know. It was like the perfect night, and now I just feel like an idiot. Did I really think someone like him would like someone like me?"

"Hey, knock that off or I'm kicking you out."

Cleo leaned forward and put her head in her hands. "What's wrong with me?"

"Nothing. If anything, this makes you normal. I've been waiting for forever for you to be interested in someone."

"Well, this isn't fun."

"Blah. He's stupid. Boys are stupid."

"Hey," a voice called out from the doorway to the bedroom.

Cleo looked up quickly to see Elle's boyfriend, Brad, standing there with his arms crossed and a pout on his face.

"We're talking about boys, babe. You're a *man.*"

Cleo watched as Brad smiled and stood a little taller, puffing out his chest before heading to the kitchen. Elle winked at her before rolling her eyes. They both giggled.

"So, you're having boy troubles, Cleo?" said Brad, as he rummaged through the fridge.

"She's been seeing a professional athlete," said Elle.

"I'd hardly call it *seeing*," said Cleo.

"Anyone I know?" Brad leaned against the counter and took a bite of pasta from a Tupperware.

"Yeah, what *is* his name?" Elle nudged Cleo.

"Kenny. Kenny Matthews."

"Ah, the shortstop. Dang, girl. You got game." Brad looked at her impressed.

"Hardly. He and his roommate basically hired me to cater an event. That's all it was."

"Yeah, but he wiped flour off her face in a seductive way," Elle chimed in and wiggled her eyebrows at Brad.

Brad raised his eyebrows as he swallowed another bite. He looked at Cleo with pride.

"It was not seductive." Cleo laughed, shoving her friend.

"Sounds seductive," said Brad.

"I'm going home." Cleo took a last bite of ice cream before putting it on the coffee table. She stood up and shook her head at the two of them. She walked past the kitchen to the door, grabbing her purse from the counter. Elle stood and followed behind, stopping in the kitchen to grab Brad's fork. She took a bite of pasta.

"Don't give up on this guy yet." She waved her fork at Cleo, her mouth full.

"Yeah, please don't. I'd love season tickets," said Brad enthusiastically.

"Brad!" Cleo gave him a playful shove.

"What? It's worth a shot." He shrugged before taking back his fork.

Cleo couldn't help but laugh. She looked at the two of them and smiled. She loved Brad for Elle, and was so happy they had found each other. It might not be as saucy as Elle would want, but their relationship was steady and loving, like an old married couple. It was exactly what Cleo wanted. She felt a little pang in her heart over Kenny, but tried to ignore it. That would never be them. That was clear after tonight.

Elle walked over and gave her a big hug. "Are you sure you don't want to stay the night? We could have a slumber party like the old days."

"Hey, what about me?" asked Brad, concerned.

"You can sleep on the couch," said Elle.

"It's okay. I'll be okay. Thanks, though." Cleo reached out and hugged Elle, and saw a look of relief spread across Brad's face.

"Text me if you need anything, okay?" Elle hugged her back tightly.

"Okay, thanks."

Cleo opened the door and waved a quick goodbye before walking down the hallway to the stairs. She already felt better. It was amazing what good friends could do. On the drive home, she listened to some feel-good music, and had almost forgotten the night at Kenny's. Almost.

As she opened the door to her house and walked into the kitchen, she was reminded of what she truly wanted. She knew this was probably for the best. She had her dream to focus on. This party was the first big step to getting there. It would hopefully get her name out there and open doors that were shut before. She would treat this party and Kenny solely as business, which it was. Once it was over, she wouldn't have to see him again.

She was going to open up that bakery, and nothing was going to get in the way of that. Especially not some guy. Besides, it wasn't like they were in a relationship. Not even close. They were friends. Not even that. They were business associates. That's it.

Chapter 14

Kenny

Kenny woke up groggily and forced his eyes open to the sunlight pouring through the floor-to-ceiling window. He groaned as he rolled over and looked out over the city. It was already awake with people walking the sidewalks with the morning coffee, heading to work with their heads down. He could hear the taxis honking in the busy traffic of the streets. New York was definitely louder than Boston.

He had driven up to see Justin on a whim, after he had left Cleo sitting speechless in the kitchen. He needed the long drive to clear his head. While he drove, he wondered what was wrong with him. He took a perfectly good night and ruined it in a second because... what? He was having a good time with a woman? A good woman. He shook his head as he thought about what an ass he had been.

He kept replaying her face in his head when he had gotten up so abruptly. The hurt that filled her eyes that she tried to hide, but failed at. The surprise that parted her lips as she watched him go. He had willed himself to keep walking without turning back because he knew if he looked at her for one more moment, he would cave. He didn't know what he would be caving into, but he was scared.

He arrived at Justin's at two in the morning, much to his friend's surprise, who groggily answered his phone.

"Kenny? Do you know what time it is?"

"Yeah. Hey. I'm sorry, man. I'm actually downstairs. Can you let me in?"

"Wait. You're here? In New York?"

"Yeah."

"I'll be right down."

Kenny had waited ten minutes and almost called back, fearful his friend had fallen back asleep. Finally, he saw Justin exit the elevators in a black robe, rubbing his eyes. He made his way to the large glass doors and used his keycard to unlock them. He pushed open the door and looked at Kenny confused.

"Surprise?" Kenny shrugged.

"Get in." Justin shook his head.

Kenny followed him to the elevators and rode up in silence to the top floor. The doors opened to a loft-style penthouse with exposed brick and modern finishes.

"Go to bed, Kenny. Explain in the morning." Justin treaded slowly down the hallway to his bedroom, shutting the door behind him.

Kenny headed to one of the guest bedrooms and collapsed onto the bed. He was tired and fell asleep almost instantly with Cleo's face running through his mind.

Now he was awake in another city, wondering what the hell he was thinking driving into the night to escape her. He heard a knock at the door and sat up in bed.

Justin opened the door, holding a hot cup of coffee.

"Hey."

"Hey. Care to explain what's going on?" Justin handed him the cup of coffee.

Kenny took it thankfully and took a long sip, closing his eyes and letting the warmth run down his throat. He could use ten more of these.

"Sorry for just showing up like that."

"It's fine. I'm just wondering what's going on with you."

"I had to get out of Boston for a little bit."

"Why? Is it the team?"

"No, no." Kenny shook his head.

"It's that girl, isn't it? The one from the café."

"I blew it, man. She'll probably never talk to me again."

"I'm sure it's not that bad." Justin glanced at his watch. He was already dressed for work in a pressed navy suit.

"It's all right if you need to go. Is it okay if I crash here for the night?"

"Stay as long as you'd like. I'm sorry to jet off like this in the midst of your woman trouble, but I have an important meeting."

Kenny waved him off, taking another sip of coffee.

"Let's go out tonight. Dinner and drinks. Get your mind off things," said Justin.

"That would be great."

After Justin left for work a few minutes later, Kenny padded out to the kitchen to make breakfast. He was starving. He made eggs and bacon, and leaned against the counter inhaling bites. He cleaned up the dishes and went back to the bedroom, where he passed out facedown on the plush bed. After sleeping for two hours, he woke up feeling better. At least more rested.

He picked up his phone, hoping there would be a text from Cleo, but was disappointed to see nothing. Did he really think she was going to talk to him? Just then his phone vibrated. It was a text from Nico:

Hey. You didn't come home last night.

Kenny: *Yeah. I'm in New York.*

Nico: *Wait, what?*

Kenny: *I just needed to get away for a bit.*

Nico: *What happened last night? You kinda left me in an awkward situation with Cleo.*

Kenny: *I know. I'm sorry, man.*

Nico: *I'm fine. Her on the other hand...*

Kenny: *That bad, huh?*

Nico: *She looked like a sad puppy dog.*

Kenny let out a sigh, rubbing his hands on his face. He had really messed this up. He picked up his phone to reply:

Shit.

Nico: *Yeah. What about practice today?*

Kenny: *Can you cover for me?*

Nico: *Are you serious?*

Kenny: *Yeah, I'm going to hang here for a bit. Just say I'm sick or something.*

Nico: *You owe me.*

Kenny: *I know. Thanks.*

Kenny locked his phone and tossed it next to him on the bed. He put on a movie and zoned out, trying to distract himself from what Nico said about Cleo.

That night, Justin took him out to a popular sushi restaurant. The place was packed and it didn't look like there were any tables, but the hostess worked her magic and sat them at a private table near the sushi bar. They ordered sake bombs and basically every roll on the menu. Kenny had never tasted anything so good.

He sat back appreciatively, taking a sip of beer and catching his breath.

"Good, huh?"

"I got to hand it to New York. They know how to do food."

"They also know how to do drinks. I'll take you to a bar after this. It will blow your mind."

"Thanks for doing this, man."

"What?"

"Taking me in like a stray. Hell, I didn't even show up with clothes or anything." Kenny brushed his hands down the lapel of the suit Justin lent him.

Justin waved him off. "You're my best friend."

After dinner, Justin's driver took them a few blocks away to what looked like a telephone booth. Kenny looked around confused as they got out of the car. Justin opened the door to the telephone booth and picked up the phone, looking at Kenny mischievously. He turned and whispered a few words, and soon the floor was vibrating. Kenny grabbed the walls of the booth, wondering if there was an earthquake. Soon, the busy street disappeared from view as they traveled down. The booth was an elevator.

It came to a gentle stop and through the glass windows, there was a large bar dimly lit up by crystal chandeliers and plush, black velvet booths surrounding it. A jazz band was playing in the corner.

"Okay. This is impressive," said Kenny.

Justin smiled knowingly, pushing the door open. They walked to the bar and took a seat, ordering whiskey drinks that were served under glass domes that when lifted, smoke poured out. They clinked their glasses.

A few drinks later, Kenny felt numb and happy. He might even find a girl tonight. It had been a while since he had been in New York. A smoking-hot redhead in an emerald-green dress sidled up next to him at the bar.

"You're a long way from home, mister," she said casually before ordering a drink.

"Am I?" asked Kenny curiously.

The redhead held out her hand. "Tinsley. Tinsley Erin. Sports radio."

Kenny shook her hand and smiled. "It's nice to put a face to a name."

He introduced her to Justin, and they all clinked their glasses together. They spent the next hour talking sports. She actually knew what she was talking about, which normally would be a turn-on for Kenny. Hell, just her appearance was a turn-on for him.

As he watched her talk energetically and felt his eyes wander to her plump lips, he thought about how this could get messy. He didn't get involved with people in the industry. Still, it was nice to get his mind off Cleo. At closing time, she linked her arm through his and they made their way back up to the street.

"Where to next, boys?" She smiled seductively.

Justin looked at Kenny to decide what move he was going to make.

"This is where I leave you, Tinsley. After I make sure you have a safe way home."

She looked up at him disappointedly and stuck out her bottom lip.

"I'm three sheets to the wind, and I don't need you talking about me on the radio." Kenny winked as he hailed a cab. He helped her inside and shut the door.

"The only thing I'll say is that you are quite the gentleman," said Tinsley, leaning out the window and kissing him on the cheek before her taxi drove away.

"Wow." Justin looked at him with a raised brow. "That baker girl really has you wrapped up."

The next morning, Kenny woke up with a pounding headache. He reached over to the nightstand and chugged a bottle of water. He groaned in pain as he vowed off whiskey for the foreseeable future. Slowly, he stumbled out to the hallway and walked to the living room. Justin was passed out on the couch and he laughed, which stirred him from his sleep.

"Whiskey. Never again," said Justin, facedown into the couch seat.

Kenny plopped down next to him. "You did promise me a good time, and you delivered."

"Yeah, but at what cost? I'm just lucky it's the weekend. I could not work in this state." Justin sat up slowly and rubbed his eyes.

Kenny leaned his head back and stared at the ceiling.

"I still can't believe you turned down that sportscaster. She was into you."

"Yeah, but I don't want to mix business with pleasure."

"That...or you're still hung up on that girl back in Boston."

"Or that. But like I said, I messed it up."

"I'm sure it's fixable."

"I don't know."

Justin hesitated for a moment. "Maybe it's time you let go of what happened with Sylvie."

"I don't want to talk about it."

"I know you don't, but maybe you need to. Just get it all out, so you can move on."

"I said I don't want to talk about it." Kenny could feel himself getting irritated.

"If this girl has you all tied up in knots then maybe she's worth pursuing."

Kenny got up from the couch to let Justin know the conversation was over. Justin put his hands up in defeat and headed to the kitchen. He came back with two glasses of water and some Advil. Kenny took it appreciatively. He felt bad for his attitude, but when it came to Sylvie, it was a sore subject.

"I know you're trying to help. I just don't know if I'm ready."

"Okay."

"I think I better head back tonight. I'm sure my coach is livid, based on the string of unread texts from Nico."

"Probably a good idea. You're a bad influence." Justin groaned and held a hand to his head.

Kenny laughed as he went to the bathroom to wash up. They headed to lunch for some hangover food and a little hair of the dog. When they were both feeling better, they went over some of Kenny's investments to see how things were going. By the time they were finished, it was already 9 p.m., and Kenny had to make the drive back home. He could not miss another practice.

The drive back to Boston went by quickly and he was thankful his hangover was subsiding. When he made it into the city, he found himself driving through it and into the suburbs. He didn't know what his next move was, but he had to see Cleo.

Chapter 15

Cleo

Cleo glanced at the clock on the wall. It was 12 a.m. She yawned and shook her head to wake herself up. There were still two more hours before closing time. She should have accepted Bridget's offer earlier when she was placing a coffee order for the staff.

She didn't know if it was the rainy weather that was making her tired, or that fact that she'd had two sleepless nights since the incident with Kenny at his condo. She couldn't help replaying the night in her head and trying to understand what happened. It was driving her crazy. She was not about to text him and ask him. She would look like a total fool. Although, she did miss texting him. She always lit up at his good morning texts or his random memes throughout the day.

She pulled her phone out of her pocket and sighed disappointedly, seeing there were no notifications. Just then she saw a few guys from the team walk in, including that creep Kev. She eyed him with dread, but was happy to see Nico walk in behind him. He gave her a little wave and a smile. For a second her heart skipped in hopes that Kenny was with them. But the door shut behind Nico. There was no one else. She bit her cheek in disappointment as Bridget sat them at their normal table.

Besides them being there, the bar was pretty quiet. It was a nice change of pace, but Cleo would have appreciated some more business as a distraction. Now that some of his teammates were here, it was going to be impossible not to think of Kenny.

Bridget walked up and leaned against the bar, looking at their table. "I wasn't expecting them tonight."

"Neither was I," said Cleo.

"Looks like they brought the creep with them." Bridget shook her head.

Cleo bit her lip nervously, and glanced over at their table.

Kev was looking right at her with that stupid smirk of his. She cleared her throat in disgust.

"Don't worry. I'll deal with them tonight. You won't have to go anywhere near him."

"Thank you," said Cleo, fighting back a yawn.

"Are you okay?"

"Yeah. Just a little tired. I should have taken you up on that iced coffee earlier."

"You look exhausted, and I don't mean that in a bad way, but in an 'I'm worried about you' way." Bridget put her hand on her shoulder.

"I'm sorry. I probably look like a wreck." Cleo brushed her hand through her hair self-consciously,

Bridget waved her off. "I don't care what you *look* like. I care about how you're feeling."

"I'll be fine." Cleo gave her boss a reassuring smile.

Bridget glanced around the bar for a moment before turning back to Cleo. "Why don't you head out early? Catch up on some sleep."

"I couldn't do that. The team just got here. What if it picks up?"

"We'll be fine. Alex is here. We've got it handled."

Cleo looked around unsurely.

"I'm serious. Go. With the game this weekend, I'll need my favorite bartender awake and ready to take on the crowd."

"Okay. Thanks, Bridget." She gave her a quick hug before heading to the back kitchen. She would have said goodbye to Nico, but not at the chance of seeing Kev. Plus, things still felt a little awkward since the other night. She wondered if Nico had talked to Kenny about it.

Probably. It had been two nights and they were roommates. She shook her head in embarrassment just thinking about it.

In the kitchen, she removed her apron and placed it in the wash pile. She waved a quick goodbye to the cooks and slipped out the back door to the alley where her car was parked and yawned as she climbed in. She definitely needed sleep and was grateful for Bridget letting her go early.

The drive home went by fast. She pulled into the driveway and pressed the button to open her garage. She waited as it slowly opened before pulling in and putting the car in park. Home sweet home. She couldn't wait to take a hot shower and climb into bed. She was about to close the garage when she heard a car pull up.

Who the hell would be here at this hour? Nervously, she peered out of the garage, but headlights blinded her. She was about to run inside and lock the door, but then the lights cut and she saw a black sports car. Kenny's car. She couldn't believe what she was seeing. She must be so tired she was hallucinating.

She combed her hands through her hair really quickly and smoothed her wrinkled bar shirt. Why did he always show up when she looked like a hot mess? She walked out of the garage as he opened the car door and stepped out. Hat on, messy hair, sweats that hugged his muscles. He was looking at her so intently and suddenly he was taking strong strides toward her. She shifted her feet and swallowed, but her throat was dry.

Cleo attempted to say "hi," but his mouth was suddenly on hers. His hands were in her hair. She knew she should pull away and ask him what the hell his problem was, but his lips were moving against hers and it felt too good. They could talk later.

She stood on her tiptoes, leaning in to him, and wrapping her arms around his neck. His hands moved to her waist as he pulled her in tighter. She could feel his fingers digging gently into her as if he was holding on for dear life. His tongue trailed across her lips, parting them patiently. She opened her mouth and breathed him in, and soon he was massaging his tongue against hers not so patiently. She felt him groan, the vibrations traveling through her, making her tingle with pleasure.

With her hands still around his neck, she pulled him with her as she walked backward into the garage, their mouths never leaving each other. Her back was soon against the door and she lowered a hand to search for the door handle. She fumbled for a little bit until she found it and turned it. The door swung open and they stumbled inside. They broke apart and she looked up at him. They were both breathing heavy, and he was staring intently back at her.

She bit her bottom lip before grabbing his hand and pulling him through the kitchen and to the stairs. She hoped he was in the mood for a shower. When they came to the bedroom, he stopped, but she shook her head and pulled him with her. He looked at her curiously, but followed without hesitating. When they reached the bathroom, she flipped the switch and he looked at her with a smile that melted her right there on the spot. She let go of his hand and turned on the shower.

Once the water was running, he came up behind her and put his hands on her waist, turning her to face him. She looked up at him nervously. She knew what was coming next. As much as she wanted it, she was also scared. It had been so long. As if he knew what she was thinking, he put his hand gently on her chin. He tilted her head up and kissed her softly.

His fingers trailed down her face, her neck, her arms, her waist, until they stopped to grab the bottom of her shirt. He pulled it up slowly and she lifted her arms as he slid it up and over her head. He looked down at her large breasts and sucked in a breath. She wanted to cover up. She knew she was probably plumper than what he was used to. When she put her hands over her stomach, he shook his head and gently pulled them away.

"Don't," he said softly, but sternly.

She did as she was told and held her hands at her sides as his eyes grazed over her admiringly. He went in to kiss her again and his hands traveled to her breasts, cupping them against her black bra. His fingers grazed the cup of her bra and pulled it down until his hands were against her. His mouth traveled down her neck and across her collarbone until he was breathing against her. Her nipples were hard as he ran his tongue over them. She let out a little moan.

Steam was escaping the shower, enveloping them. It was hard to catch her breath. His mouth still on her, and his hands traveled down and unbuttoned her jeans with ease. He pulled them down and she shimmied herself out of them, her panties following. He stood up and looked down at her as his hands unhooked her bra, allowing it to fall to the floor.

She held his gaze as her hands reached to his sweatshirt, tugging at it roughly. He let out a soft laugh as he pulled it up over his head. She let out a small gasp as she took him in. His skin was tan and his stomach muscular. His pants hung low, revealing a perfect V. She grabbed the waistband and pulled them slowly down, his erection popping out. He stepped out of his pants, kicking them away impatiently.

Not turning away from him, she pulled open the shower door and stepped inside. The hot water washed over her, turning her sensations up a notch. The steam rose, surrounding her. She could barely see. She heard the shower door close softly and felt him step beside her. She sucked in a breath, waiting for what came next.

His hands guided her toward the shower wall, and he pressed her up against it gently. His fingers intertwined with hers and guided her hands up above her head. With one hand, Kenny pinned them there as his other hand traveled slowly down her wet body. She shuddered as he passed her stomach and stopped between her legs. He massaged his palm against her, slowly and with ease, the water allowing him to slide against her.

Cleo rested her head against the shower wall and looked up at his strong hand holding hers. Then she felt a finger slip into her slowly and gasped. She lowered her head and looked at him suddenly through the steam. He had a smile on his lips as he slowly pulled his finger out before dipping back into her. She leaned forward and pressed her lips against his desperately. Their tongues danced around each other madly, and his finger inside her matched the rhythm.

She moaned into his open mouth, the water pouring over them. Cleo pulled her hands free and reached down, taking his erection in her hand. She began moving her hand up and down and felt him grow harder, which filled her with satisfaction. She slid over him with ease, moving faster. As he pulled away from her, she felt his breath speed up. Hunger was in his eyes.

Kenny gripped her hips and spun her around, placing her hands on the shower wall. His hands moved up her sides and grabbed her breasts. She could feel his breath on her neck before his tongue trailed up to her earlobe. She leaned her head back against him.

His hands were suddenly at her hips again, gripping them roughly as she felt the tip of his erection against her. He slid into her slowly, filling her. She let out a loud moan and pushed back into him, feeling every inch. He slid out of her before thrusting back into her faster this time. She held her hands firmly against the shower wall as he continued pumping inside of her. His hand reached around, and he massaged his fingers against her. Her eyes rolled back before she shut them tight, feeling herself close to the edge. His fingers moved faster against her as he pulled out and pushed into her again frantically. She exploded around him as he throbbed inside her before swiftly pulling out. She spun around slowly, looking up at him with exhausted pleasure. He leaned down and kissed her before pressing his forehead against hers.

Chapter 16

Kenny

Kenny woke up and smiled as he looked around. The sun was just pouring through the sheer white curtains and the walls were painted a pale yellow. He turned his head to see Cleo sleeping soundly next to him. He watched her for a moment, listening to her breathing and stirring slightly as if she was dreaming. He felt like he was dreaming to be waking up here, next to her.

Last night had been one of the best he's ever had. It was spontaneous and passionate and unlike anything he'd ever felt before. When he had left New York, he had no idea he would end up here. It was almost like instinct. His hands turned the steering wheel and his foot pressed the brake where it needed to, as he followed his memory to Cleo's house.

It had been late. Really late. But lucky for him, she had been working that night and showing up in the early hours of the morning didn't matter. When he had turned down her street, he had gone over what he might say. How could he explain himself for his abrupt exit the other night? How could he explain he was damaged goods, but somehow was drawn to her? Except when he saw her, the words escaped him. He let his mouth do the talking.

The shower had been unexpected. Everything had been. She was so much more beautiful than he could ever imagined with her soft, supple skin and curves he could gently dig his fingers into. The way she was unnecessarily self-conscious when he took her clothes off. He hoped he had done his job in reassuring her there was absolutely nothing to worry about.

They moved to the bedroom, but did not sleep for hours. They didn't talk either, which was what made the morning that much more difficult because he had to leave now. He had an early morning meeting with his coach to talk about his sudden absence the past few days. He couldn't miss it.

He watched her sleep a little while longer, before gently pulling his arm out from under her. She stirred slightly, but then gently snored and was back in a deep sleep. He pushed the sheets off him and slowly climbed out of the bed. It was difficult to leave the cloud of blankets and the warmth of her body. He searched for his clothes and pulled them on swiftly. He leaned down and kissed her on the cheek before walking carefully out the door, closing it behind him.

As much as he'd like to skip this morning meeting of being chewed out by his coach, it was probably better this way. When she woke up, she would probably want to talk about everything. He still didn't know what to say or how to explain anything. He would probably say something that would hurt her, and he couldn't bear to see that look on her face again. She probably didn't want to hear "I want you, but I don't want you" or "I'm not looking for anything serious, but last night was fun" or "I'm scared of getting hurt again." He had a lot to sort through.

Krnny walked down the stairs and looked around for something to write a note on. He wasn't going to just leave without a word. He wasn't a monster. A note felt more personal than a text. He looked around and found a pad of paper near her recipe books in the kitchen. He smiled as he read her notes on a new cake recipe. Her passion for baking was a turn-on. It meant she had her own thing going on. Her own brain. Her own dreams.

He found a pen in a drawer and jotted down something down quickly:

Thank you for last night. I'm sorry I had to leave. Talk soon.

He left it near her coffeemaker and walked to the front door, taking in his surroundings before he left. He hoped he would be here again, but couldn't feel confident. He climbed into his car and turned the key in the ignition, hoping it wouldn't wake her. Sports cars were sleek, but a little noisy. He pulled out of the driveway and drove home. It was early enough to take a shower and prepare for his meeting.

His coach had texted him late last night:

8 AM. Tomorrow. My office.

It wasn't a question.

Kenny arrived home to a quiet house. Nico must have still been sleeping. He took a hot shower and couldn't help but think about last night in Cleo's bathroom. It would have been a much better shower if she was here with him, but he would definitely be late. After his shower he dried off and put on some workout clothes. He might as well get a workout in at the gym, since he would be over there anyway. Maybe a sweat session would help him clear his head.

He walked to the kitchen and put a pot of coffee on, then leaned against the counter and breathed in the aroma of coffee beans that filled the air. Sliding his phone out of his pocket, he checked if there was any text from her, but there was nothing. He breathed a little sigh of relief. She was probably still sleeping.

He heard someone clear their throat and saw Nico shuffle slowly into the kitchen. Kenny gave him a nod before pouring himself a cup of coffee.

"Want a cup?"

"Yes, please," said Nico as he sat at the counter and groggily put his head in his hands.

"Late night?"

"Yeah. I really have to limit my nights out."

"Probably a good idea with the big game coming up."

"And what about you? Where have you been?"

"I drove back from New York late last night." Kenny hoped he wouldn't ask too many questions.

"I didn't hear you get in."

"I'm sure you don't remember much of anything." Kenny shrugged.

"That's true." Nico laughed. "Did you talk to coach yet?"

"I'm meeting with him at eight. How bad was he?"

"He was pretty pissed, especially with the game so soon. I told him you were sick, so stick with that or both of our asses will be in hot water."

"Thanks, man. I owe you." Kenny raised his coffee mug before taking a sip.

"You'd better go," said Nico, checking his phone for the time. "You don't want to piss him off any more."

"True. I'll see you at practice later."

Kenny downed his coffee and grabbed his keys before heading down to the parking garage. There was still no text from Cleo, which was bothering him way more than he wished it would. He had other things to focus on, like making things right with his coach so he could start next game. Maybe this was why he didn't get too close to women. Relationships were too complicated and distracting.

He arrived just before eight and clambered up the stairs to his coach's office, who was sitting in his brown leather chair with his back turned. Kenny swallowed hard before knocking lightly. His coach spun around quickly and waved him in.

"Glad to see you're alive," he said sarcastically.

"Yes, sir. I'm sorry for missing practice the past few days."

"You take this game seriously, don't you, Kenny?"

"Of course, sir. It's my life."

"Well, clearly not your whole life or you would have been here, and not in New York."

Kenny looked taken aback.

His coach nodded knowingly. "I know all about your partying in the Big Apple when you should have been here."

"H-how?" stammered Kenny.

"You were the talk of sports radio this morning. You seemed to make an impression on that Tinsley woman."

Kenny looked down at his feet, feeling ashamed. He should have known.

"She said all good things. In fact, she said you were one of the more respectable players she'd met."

Kenny looked at his coach with a hopeful expression.

"While this looks good for our team's reputation, I'm still pissed," his coach continued. "Now I don't know what's going on with you, but if you can't get your head in the game then I can't start you."

"Please, sir. It won't happen again. I just needed to blow off some steam."

"Everything all right?"

"Yes. Everything is fine now. Again, that will be the last time I blow off practice."

His coach studied him for a minute before sighing in defeat. "Fine. Don't be late for practice today."

"I won't, sir." Kenny started for the door before turning around.

"Yes?"

"Don't be too hard on Nico."

His coach rolled his eyes and waved him away.

Kenny rode the elevator up to the fitness level. There wasn't anyone there, which wasn't unusual given there was practice later. He was happy to be alone. He grabbed a towel and a water bottle from the locker room before hopping on the treadmill. He checked his phone, but there was nothing from Cleo. He scrolled to his music app and put on a workout playlist.

He began with a speed walk, then a jog, and then sprints. The music and the movement helped, but he couldn't get his mind fully off of his night with Cleo, which frustrated him. Kenny increased the speed and ran faster, beating his last time that his trainer had recorded. He smiled to himself thinking about the smug look Kev had given him about their times. He hit the stop button after thirty minutes and caught his breath.

Heading to the locker room he undressed, shoving everything in his locker. He grabbed a towel and wrapped it around his waist before turning the sauna on. Once it heated up, he stepped inside, laid down on the warm wood, and closed his eyes.

As much as he tried to fight them, his thoughts brought him back to Cleo's house when they had just finished in the shower. He had wrapped her up in a fluffy white towel before doing the same and carrying her to her bedroom. They had lain in comfortable silence for a few minutes, catching their breaths after their steamy shower.

It would have the perfect time to talk about what had happened. He knew he owed her an explanation after he ruined a perfectly good night. At one point, she had even rolled over and looked at him as if she was about to ask, but as soon as she opened her mouth to speak, he pressed his lips against hers and they started up again. When they were finished for the second time, they were so tired they passed out. Lucky for him.

He knew he couldn't avoid her forever or come onto her anytime she tried to talk, although he wouldn't mind doing the latter again. And again. Still, Cleo was a good girl. He knew it deep down, which was probably why he was so drawn to her. But it was probably also why he needed to avoid her. He didn't want to hurt her.

Kenny rubbed his palm against his forehead in frustration. What had he done? He had made a mistake by sleeping with her. Now there were probably feelings on her end, and he was in no position to be handling anyone's feelings. At least, not with proper care. He hadn't felt this protective of anyone since Sylvie, and now he was the one Cleo needed protecting from. If he tried to explain it, she wouldn't understand. No one did. Years had passed, and he still couldn't get over the past.

Even if Cleo was perfect for him, which he was pretty positive she was, he couldn't trust himself not to break her heart. How was he supposed to get through Mae's birthday party, knowing she would be there? It wasn't like he could skip it. He lived there. He would have to face her eventually.

Chapter 17

Cleo

Cleo opened her eyes slowly, stretching her arms out to find that no one was beside her. She rolled over quickly to see that the bed was empty beside her. She knew this would happen. Still, she couldn't help but feel a little disappointed. Okay, a lot disappointed that Kenny was gone.

After the night they had, she hoped he would still be here. She pulled a pillow over her head to shut out the light and try to shut out the thoughts from last night. A pillow couldn't stop her from remembering his lips on hers, his hands gripping her hips, the hot water rolling down his skin pressed up against hers. When she had pleasured herself in the shower a week ago, she had no idea what would come to be in that same spot.

The sex was better than she even imagined. The way he looked at her made her feel beautiful, even though she knew she was anything but. He had made her feel comfortable, confident even. No one had ever done that. He must have been a really good actor or a total sociopath for dipping out on her. She groaned into the pillow, but it smelled like him, which pissed her off more.

She threw it off her and reached over to her nightstand. Maybe he had texted her. She powered it on. It must have died in the night because she hadn't charged it. It lit up, but there were no notifications. More disappointment. She set it back on her nightstand before sliding out of bed. She rummaged through her dresser drawers and found some sweats to put on. All she wanted to do was curl up into a little ball on the couch, which she would, but she needed breakfast first.

Cleo walked past her bathroom and saw towels and her work clothes strewn across the floor. She quickly shut the door, ignoring the proof that last night had happened. Once she was downstairs, she opened the fridge and pulled out eggs and bacon. She fired up the stove and began cooking. The pan sizzled and popped, and the smells in the kitchen made her stomach grumble. It was eleven after all, and she had worked up quite an appetite last night.

She walked over to pull a plate down from the cabinet, and that was when she saw it. A little yellow post-it note sitting next to her recipe books. She quickly picked it up and read it.

Thank you for last night.

Was he really thanking her? Like it was a favor?

I'm sorry I had to leave.

Doubtful.

Talk soon.

Also doubtful. Also, how could he be so nonchalant? He had just as good a time as she did. She might not be the most beautiful girl he had been with, but she could see and feel how good of a time he was having. She almost smiled, thinking of the way he shuddered against her as he came, but then she remembered he had left. He got what he wanted from her. As much as it hurt, it wasn't all that surprising.

She read the note again before crumpling it up and throwing it in the trash. She filled her plate with eggs, bacon, and buttered toast and sat down at the kitchen table to eat. Her phone vibrated in her pocket. She slid it out quickly, but it was only Bridget:

Big game tonight. I hope you're rested because the bar is going to be packed. If you need the night off, tell me now, so I can maybe get Alex in.

It was game night? Cleo groaned. She had forgotten. The last place she wanted to be was in a bar full of TV screens with Kenny's face on it and people cheering him on. Still, she didn't want to let Bridget down, especially after the favor last night. Plus, the money was good.

Cleo: *All good here. Thanks again. I'll be there.*

Bridget: *Thanks, Cleo! See you at 5.*

Cleo locked her phone and put it on the table. She took a bite of bacon. At least she had a while before she had to be at work. She could still curl up on the couch and watch bad TV, which was the ultimate comfort.

Then it hit her. Game night. The team usually came in after the game. No, no. This was not good. What if Kenny came in? How could she face him? It would be so embarrassing. Worse, what if he told the team? She would be just another conquest they would high-five over. No, Kenny wasn't like that. As much as he hurt her by leaving her, he didn't seem like that kind of guy. She would just have to deal with it. It was her own fault for getting involved with someone she saw on a somewhat regular basis.

For the rest of the afternoon, she made herself feel better by baking a batch of her favorite sea salt chocolate chip cookies and sitting on the couch with a big knit blanket wrapped around her. She watched her favorite reality TV show, booing at the romance and laughing at the drama. She was about to start another episode when there was a knock on the door.

She started. Her first thought was maybe it was Kenny. If it was, she was not going to answer it looking like this. Setting the remote down, and keeping the blanket wrapped around her like a shawl, she tiptoed to the door. Who could it be? She wasn't expecting anyone or any packages. She tried to peek out the window.

"I can see you in there."

Cleo breathed a sigh of relief. It was Elle.

"Open up."

Cleo unlocked the door and opened it.

Elle looked her up and down with amusement. "Well, this is a look."

"Shut up." Cleo waved her inside. Elle slid past her and into the living room, and plopped down on the couch. Cleo sat next to her.

"Uh-oh," said Elle, spotting the plate of cookies.

"What?"

"You only bake those when you're sad or homesick."

"Do not."

"Do too. And what's with the blanket? You look like an old cat lady."

Cleo pulled it off her head and tossed it on the couch.

"And you're watching *this*?" Elle asked.

Cleo nodded. "You have murder mysteries. I have this."

"Well, according to the evidence, this looks like the scene of a breakup."

"I'd have to have a boyfriend for a breakup," said Cleo softly.

"True," said Elle, studying her for a moment. "Oh no. What happened with the shortstop?"

As much as Cleo wanted to keep last night and this morning's humiliation to herself, she couldn't. She burst into tears and told Elle everything. Elle pulled her in for a big hug as she listened intently. When Cleo finally caught her breath, Elle held her out at arm's length and looked at her with a fire blazing in her eyes.

"Where's the note?" she asked.

"In the garbage."

"And he didn't even text or call to check in? What if you hadn't seen it?"

Cleo shook her head.

"What an asshole. I'm so sorry, Cleo."

Cleo shrugged defeatedly.

They sat in silence for a little bit before a small smile creeped over Elle's face.

"At least you can say you got it on with a pro baseball player."

"Elle!" Cleo shouted, shoving her friend.

"What?"

Cleo laughed softly.

"How was it?"

"Elle!"

"I'm just curious!"

"I don't kiss and tell." Cleo couldn't help but smile. Thinking about the sex, without the tarnish of the morning, made her blush.

"Oh, my God!" Elle pointed at her. "It was good."

"Amazing." Cleo sighed dramatically, falling back into the couch.

Elle fell beside her as they looked up at the ceiling.

"Well, at least you got some. It's been a while."

"Shut up." Cleo tossed a throw pillow at her friend.

She was happy Elle was here. She was already feeling a little better. They spent the next hour watching another episode of reality TV and finishing the plate of cookies.

"I better go," said Elle, getting up from the couch.

"Yeah. I need to get ready for work."

"Text me if you need anything."

"Thanks, Elle. Really."

"Anytime." Elle hugged her before heading out the front door.

Cleo made her way upstairs and pushed open the bathroom door. She gathered her clothes and walked them to the laundry room, tossing them in the hamper. When she opened the shower door, she swore she could smell him. *She* smelled like him. She washed her hair and scrubbed her skin quickly before getting out and toweling off. He had ruined her shower for her.

"Curse you, Kenny," she muttered.

She finished getting ready for work, without putting too much effort into it. She didn't want to look like she was trying too hard in case he did show up. She wore her wet hair in a low bun, and her usual jeans and T-shirt.

She got to work right on time and saw that it was already packed. The game was coming on in an hour. She was thankful for the business because it was a good distraction, even though his face was going to come on all ten television screens soon. Maybe she would make it a game by trying to expertly avoid looking.

The next few hours she made cocktails, poured beers, and served game day appetizers to the crowd as they cheered and booed at the game. It was a big game, so Bridget had the music turned down and the game volume up. Cleo actively tried not to look whenever she heard the announcers say Kenny's name. She had been doing a good job at avoiding looking, but her curiosity finally got the better of her.

"Kenny Matthews is up to bat, with the bases loaded," an announcer said loudly over the speakers.

She watched as he took a few practice swings. Damn him for looking so good. The camera zoomed in on his face as he squared up to the base. A little bit of sadness hit her and she forced herself to look away. She began drying glasses that were already dry. She needed something to do.

Suddenly, the bar erupted into cheers, startling her.

"Kenny Matthews hits a home run. It's a grand slam!"

She watched as Kenny ran the bases, his teammates rushing the field. Once he hit home plate, they lifted him up on their shoulders. With the excitement from the bar, and the smile on his face, she couldn't help but feel happy for him. He had won them the game.

To hers and Bridget's surprise, the team did not come in after their big win. Cleo felt a mixture of relief and disappointment. It was definitely because of her, and she felt like a complete idiot. Somehow, she made it through the night without crying. And the next.

The next few days she went through the motions, and was happy when Monday rolled around because she could just hole up inside her house for a few days. She couldn't believe that Kenny hadn't texted or called. He had gone radio silent on her.

She started feeling anxious about the party approaching. How was she going to be in the same room with him? Her heart dropped just thinking about it. She even contemplated quitting the job, but she didn't want to disappoint Nico. More importantly, she didn't want to blow her big break. She could not let some guy get in the way of her dream. But she would need reinforcements if she were going to go through with this.

She texted Elle:

Come with me to the party. I need you.

Cleo smiled at her response:

I'm there.

Chapter 18

Kenny

Kenny slammed his locker with a bang and sulked out of the locker room, his teammates casting him wary looks. He didn't care. It had been a hell of a week. First, he had crossed a line with Cleo and there was no going back. He hadn't heard from her, which wasn't surprising. He had left an excuse on a post-it, for God's sake. Still, he hoped maybe this miniscule gesture was enough for her to text him.

Besides all the stormy feelings regarding Cleo, Nate had become aware that he was his brother, which made for a very awkward and unexpected phone call. His mother had finally come clean about his father's transgressions. Despite the lost years between them, and despite Kenny's hesitancy, they actually hit it off okay.

The past week they had spent some time together after practice. Nate had taken him to lunch yesterday at a greasy diner that was known for their loaded cheeseburgers. Kenny was expecting his brother to be stuffy, but he was actually very humble, despite being a multi-millionaire. They spent hours at the diner talking about their very different childhoods and their cheater of a father.

Kenny was happy to no longer be holding on to this secret, but it did bring along a lot of curious looks from his teammates. He wasn't in the mood to answer any questions or explain his life story, so he kept his head down, which was why he wanted to get out of the locker room quickly. He took the stairs in order to avoid riding with any of his teammates in the elevator.

He found his car in the parking garage and slid into the driver's seat. His phone buzzed in his pocket. He pulled it out and saw Nate's name on the screen.

"Hello?" he answered.

"Hey, man. Do you have time to talk?"

"Uh, sure. What's up?"

"Can you meet me at Hanny's uptown?"

"What? Now?"

"Yeah."

"Sure. I'll be there in fifteen."

He hung up and tossed his phone on the seat. What could Nate want now? They'd spent most of the week getting to know each other, which was great, but Kenny was ready to just go home and unload. Despite his big win last weekend, coach had not let up on drilling them at practices.

Fifteen minutes later he pulled up to the valet at Hanny's and casually tossed the attendant his keys. He pushed through the glass door and spotted Nate at the bar sipping on a beer. Spotting him, Nate waved him over.

"I ordered you one. I figured you could use it after practice," said Nate, as Kenny took a seat beside him.

"Thanks. Coach has been working us pretty hard."

"So, I've heard from Jonas. He really thinks you guys will make it to the finals this year. That's probably why coach feels the pressure."

The bartender slid Kenny a tall, frosted glass of amber beer.

"Thank you." Kenny took a sip, before looking at Nate questioningly.

"I know you're probably sick of me, but your buddy Nico called me up. He's worried about you."

Kenny shook his head. Of course it was Nico. He had been trying to pry something out of him since everything went down with Cleo. He hadn't wanted to tell him he had screwed the caterer for his party, so he ignored his questions. It was annoying that he went behind his back and called his long-lost brother in for help. They were still getting to know each other. They weren't exactly best friends.

Filling the silence, Nate continued, "So, what's up? The team says you're like a thunder storm rolling through every day."

"It's nothing." Kenny shrugged.

"Look, I know we're just getting to know each other, but I'm your brother. I want to act like one. We've already lost so many years."

"I know. I'm sorry. I've just been dealing with some shit."

"Is it coach? The practices?"

Kenny took a sip of his beer before shaking his head. "Nah. I've been on my game. All is good with the team."

Nate studied him for a moment. "Girl trouble then?"

Kenny hesitated before answering. He had nothing to lose in telling his brother the minor details, especially since he had no idea who Cleo was.

"Yeah, you could say that."

"Ahh, I remember those days. I should have guessed when Nico told me you were basically PMSing."

Kenny rolled his eyes and couldn't help but laugh.

"So, who is she?"

"Her name's Cleo. It started off as friendly, but then we crossed a line last weekend and I panicked and bailed. I haven't talked to her since."

"Yikes." Nate grimaced and downed the rest of his beer.

"Yeah. I know."

"So, what's stopping you from calling her?"

"I don't know. I just don't think I'm ready for commitment."

"But you like the girl?"

"Yeah. A lot."

"So, call her. Text her. Whatever. It's not like you're marrying her. Just see where it goes."

"I don't know. She probably doesn't want to hear from me after I snuck out of her place."

"Look, Avery and I didn't have the smoothest of starts either, but we ended up just fine. You never know."

"Thanks, man. I appreciate it."

"Any time." Nate patted him on the back.

On the drive home, Kenny was feeling better. He wasn't ready to reach out to Cleo just yet, but that was okay. He was going to see her at the party tomorrow night. That would hopefully give him the answers he needed. Would she ignore him? Would she talk to him? Would she forgive him? Would he be ready to see where it could go?

He ran through all the different scenarios in his head and soon arrived home. Nico was in the kitchen eating a slice of pizza. He looked up at him nervously as Kenny leaned against the wall with his arms crossed.

"Look, man. Don't be pissed. I didn't know what to do. You've been such an ass lately."

"It's fine." Kenny rolled his eyes.

Nico smiled with relief.

"Are you coming out tonight?" asked Kenny, grabbing a slice of pizza.

"Yeah. What time does Justin get in?"

Kenny checked his phone for the time. "In about an hour. He's going to check in at the hotel and then head over."

"Cool. But remember, we can't go too crazy. Tomorrow's Mae's party. I'd feel lousy if I was a hungover host."

"Of course."

"It'll be nice to see Cleo, huh?"

"Yeah, I guess. I kind of forgot she would be there." Kenny lied. He finished his pizza and headed to his room to unwind before their night out. He was glad Justin was coming into town. Having his best friend around for all this Cleo and Nate drama was just what he needed.

Two hours later, the three of them called a cab and headed to a steakhouse for dinner. They ordered a nice bottle of red wine and some ribeyes with mashed potatoes and steamed broccoli.

"It's nice to be out without the rest of the team," said Nico between bites.

"Tell me about it. I was starting to get sick of them, since coach doubled up on practices."

"Everyone is saying you guys are going to go all the way this year," said Justin.

Kenny shrugged, "I don't know. Maybe. I don't want to jinx it."

"Okay, Mr. Superstitious. Where do you wanna go tonight? The usual spot?"

"No," said Kenny a little too quickly. He had successfully avoided Murphy's the past week because of the sure chance he would see Cleo behind the bar.

Nico looked at him funny.

"What if the guys are there?"

"True. If I have to see that smug look on Kev's face anymore, I might punch it straight off."

Kenny laughed out loud.

"Why don't we try that new bar that just opened? It's the same owner of the one in New York. I was in last week. It's pretty cool," said Justin.

"Sounds good."

They finished their dinners and Kenny was so stuffed he didn't think he could make it for a night out. He had eaten so much food he thought he might fall asleep right there in the booth. They decided to walk to the bar, to help their food digest.

Fifteen minutes later, they arrived. There was a line wrapped around to the back alley. Nico groaned, but the doorman waved them over.

"That was some grand slam last week," he said to Kenny, as he lifted the velvet rope to let them pass.

"Thanks, man," said Kenny, as he patted him on the back.

Inside it was packed. A clear U-shaped bar sat in the center of the room with clear barstools surrounding it. There was a DJ in the corner playing mash-ups of the popular songs on the radio right now. Most of the booths were occupied, but there were a few high-top tables open.

"I'll get the first round," said Justin, turning to the bar.

He returned shortly with a round of beers. They all took swigs, and soon Nico was making eye contact with a blonde girl on the dance floor.

"You waste no time, do you?" said Justin with a smirk.

"I'll see you boys in a little while." Nico grabbed his beer from the table and they watched him introduce himself to the girl. Soon, they were dancing.

"What about you? Anyone of interest?" asked Justin, as he looked out on the dance floor.

"Nah. I'm not looking for anything tonight."

"And why's that?"

"No reason."

"Whatever happened with that girl from the bar? The baker?"

"Nothing," Kenny lied.

Justin looked at him like he didn't believe him, but he dropped it. After a few songs, Nico came back to the table with his arm around his dance partner.

"Guys. This is Maddy. Maddy. The guys," said Nico, kissing her on the cheek.

She giggled and shook their hands.

"Do you mind if my friends join us? They just got here."

"The more the merrier," said Justin.

She looked around for her friends and squealed when she spotted them. One was tall and raven-haired, wearing a white strappy dress, and the other was a more petite blonde in jeans and a crop top. She waved them over excitedly, and they linked arms, whispering to each other when they saw the guys.

"I call dibs on the dark-haired one," said Justin quietly, nudging Kenny.

"Fine by me."

After introductions were made, Kenny quickly forgot their names. He wasn't interested. He hadn't been interested in anyone since he met Cleo. Sure, he had tried, knowing the distraction would be good for him, but nothing worked. After their night together, he didn't even try any more, much the petite blonde's dismay.

"Do you want to dance?" She leaned in, her elbows on the table, eyeing Kenny flirtatiously.

"I'm not much of a dancer," he said, taking a sip of beer.

"Oh," she said, trying to hide her disappointment.

Kenny watched Justin and Nico exchange a quick look, but they didn't say anything.

"Come dance with us!" The dark-haired girl wrapped her arm around Justin's and grabbed her friend's hand, pulling her with them. Nico and Maddy joined them, leaving Kenny alone, which was fine with him. He laughed at Justin's awkward dance moves and shook his head as he watched Nico making out like a middle schooler at a school dance.

At the end of the night, Kenny stood by as his friends exchanged numbers and then hailed a cab. The three of them piled in. They started toward Justin's hotel to drop him off before heading home.

"That's the most fun I've had in a while," said Nico, catching his breath.

"You all right there?" asked Kenny, raising an eyebrow.

"I'm winded."

"From dancing or sucking face?"

"Shut up." He slugged Kenny. "You're just jealous."

Kenny laughed and shook his head. Tonight was fun. It was just what he had needed before tomorrow's big night when he would finally see Cleo.

Chapter 19

Cleo

Cleo's kitchen counters were so full, she couldn't even see them. She sat at her kitchen table folding up white pastry boxes and lining them with tissue paper. She took her time because she wanted everything to look professional for the party tonight. She was thankful Bridget had given her the night off so she was able to take the job when Nico had offered it to her.

Folding up the boxes was a mindless task, but she took comfort in the routine of it. Unpack, fold, line. Unpack, fold, line. She tried to focus on these three steps and these three steps only. She didn't need her mind wandering to Kenny.

She had been fighting back her nerves all week as the party got closer and closer. She had hoped she would have heard from him since their night together, but there had been nothing. It had clearly been a one-night thing and she had to accept that. What had she really expected? The handsome, professional athlete would fall in love with the pudgy baker? She shook her head at her silly thoughts as she folded up the last box.

Now it was time to pack the boxes up with the pastries she had spent the past few days whipping up in the kitchen. It was quite the task for one person, especially since Nico kept adding to the guest list and receiving more RSVPs than he had intended. He had finally given her the final count three nights ago, so she could get started.

The party had gotten so big that they had to move locations to a home twenty minutes from the city. She had hoped it would have been at Nico and Kenny's condo as initially planned. She loved their kitchen and was comfortable there. Well, she was, until everything with Kenny happened. Maybe it was better this way. Their condo simply didn't have enough space, which was saying something about the size of the party.

Cleo started packing from smallest to largest. She started with the cupcakes and cookies, and ended with boxing up the individual tiers for the four-tier red velvet cake. She would assemble it there. She was arriving early to get everything set up. Thankfully, whoever owned the home was providing the trays and cake stands. All she had to do was get the pastries and cake there in one piece.

She finished placing the top tier of the cake in its box and looked around the kitchen with her hands on her hips. She was proud of herself.

This was the largest order she ever had, and she'd done it all on her own. Elle would be there in about two hours to help her pack up her car and head to the home where the party was being thrown. She was so thankful she would have her best friend there to calm her nerves. As big as this party was going to be, she knew she would still see Kenny. At least, she thought. Hoped. He couldn't avoid her (or the dessert table) forever. Or could he?

She headed upstairs to get ready. She opted to take a bubble bath in hopes it would relax her. Avoiding the shower helped too. Every time she went in there now, all she could think of was Kenny behind her, breathing in her ear and kissing her neck. Not a bad memory to have, but not one she needed to think about when she would see him tonight. It also wasn't a memory she should hold onto any longer. They were done.

She drew a hot bath, poured in some bubble bath, and sunk into the tub with a relaxing sigh. This was exactly what she needed after being on her feet for the past few days in the kitchen. She leaned her head back against the tub and closed her eyes, going over a mental checklist. Everything was ready, except for her.

Once she was finished with her bath, she wrapped herself in a towel and laid her minimal makeup collection on the counter. She put on a feel-good playlist on her phone and started to get ready. There was the usual concealer and mascara, but she added a hint of blush and winged eyeliner that took her three tries. It was finished off with a swipe of rose lipstick that would be fitting with her chef coat. After brushing out her long brown hair, she pulled it back into a low ponytail. She smiled confidently at herself before heading to her closet to get dressed.

She put on a form-fitting, knee-length dress with a pair of black ballet flats, then pulled down the pink chef's coat she had splurged on for the party tonight. It was the perfect shade of blush pink. She wanted to look the part of a chef. This was a big night after all.

Despite seeing Kenny and wanting to look good for him, she also wanted to look professional and put together for potential clients. Now that the party's guest list was bigger, there was more opportunity for her. She had her business cards ready to go and was planning on setting them near her desserts. Maybe tonight would be her big break.

The doorbell rang. Elle was early, which was fine. There was a lot to pack up in the car. Cleo glanced at herself one last time before heading downstairs.

"Wow. You look great," said Elle once Cleo opened the door.

188

"Thank you."

"Is this new?" Elle ran her hand down the sleeve of Cleo's pink chef coat.

"Mhmm.

"I love it! You look like the real deal, Cleo. I can't wait to see all those professional athletes and fancy housewives try your desserts. This is the break you've been waiting for."

"I know. I can't believe it."

"Well, let's get packing."

They spent the next twenty minutes packing the desserts into Cleo's small hatchback. It was like putting together a puzzle, trying to figure out how to stack the boxes so everything would fit. They had to be careful not to crush anything inside. Finally, they got everything in the car and Cleo held her breath as she shut the trunk door.

She climbed into the driver's seat and Elle slid into the passenger seat, which was pushed up close to the dash to make room for everything. Cleo laughed at her friend, who tried to pass off being comfortable.

"Thank you," she said, patting Elle's hand. "I couldn't do this without you."

"You could, but I'm happy to help," said Elle reassuringly.

Cleo put the car into drive and pulled out of the garage. She drove slower than usual as to not cause the desserts to slide around. Even though she had packed everything with extra care, it was better to be safe than sorry. After a forty-minute drive and a few honks from impatient drivers, she pulled up to the house.

Mansion, to be more accurate. It was a large, brick, two story with tall, white columns and white shuttered windows. There were deep green vines climbing toward the roof, which housed not one, but two chimneys. She and Elle gaped up at the house as they climbed out of the car, which looked very out of place.

"Whose place is this?" asked Elle curiously.

"I have no idea."

Just then the front door opened and Nico walked out. Spotting the girls, he gave a little wave before walking over.

"Cleo! You made it." He gave her a quick hug.

"Yes. This is my friend, er, assistant, Elle."

Nico shook Elle's hand and smiled. "Nice to meet you."

"You too. This place is beautiful," said Elle, waving toward the house.

"Right? Thankfully, one of the bigwigs had a house we could use. Here, I'll show you to the kitchen." Nico gestured to the house and began walking.

The inside was even more impressive than the outside, with a large crystal chandelier and a double staircase. As they walked, Cleo could only imagine what the kitchen looked like. When they reached it, it did not disappoint. It had white quartz countertops framed by white cabinetry with gold hardware, and a large island in the center.

"Feel free to move freely about the kitchen. The caterer will be here to set up soon and they'll be working out of the butler's pantry. I thought you could set up just outside the dining room. There is already a large table ready for you and pull whatever you need from the cabinets," said Nico.

"Thank you. This is great. We'll start bringing everything in."

It took about an hour to set up the dessert table. Cleo was glad Elle was there to give her a second opinion for the display. There were more than enough trays and cake stands to choose from. Once they were finished, they stood back and admired the table. It was grandiose, with the number of desserts sitting on crystal platters and tiered trays.

Elle put her arm around her and gave her a squeeze. "You did it, girl. Now, we just need a little champagne to celebrate. It is a party, after all."

"Elle! I'm working!" Cleo laughed.

"Did I hear champagne?" Nico walked up holding two glasses. He handed one to each of them.

"Thank you!" said Elle with no hesitation.

"You two deserve it. This looks incredible."

"Thank you," said Cleo.

Nico gave them a friendly wink before walking away. The girls clinked their glasses and sipped the champagne. Cleo felt a little more at ease as the bubbles ran down her throat.

"This is the best champagne I've ever tasted," said Elle, looking at her glass appreciatively.

They finished their champagne just as the guests began to arrive. Their first stop wasn't the dessert table. Their first stop was the bar or the appetizers set up on the other side of the room, so Cleo and Elle were able to people watch. Women in fancy cocktail dresses and men in pressed suits filled the room not only with their bodies, but also a hum of conversation.

About thirty minutes into the party, Cleo saw Kenny walk in. She felt like the air had been knocked out of her as she took him in. He was wearing a well-fitted black suit with a black tie. She had never seen him dressed up. His hair was held in place by a pomade, except for one piece that fell onto his forehead. Him and that unruly hair. He slid his hand through his hair trying to tame it with no luck.

Cleo pretended to be busy, but watched as he looked around. He skimmed over her table, careful to look only at the desserts and not her. Then he made his way to the bar. *Well, that's that*, she thought. He was avoiding her. She fought back the burning tears that were forming in her eyes.

Elle must have felt her tense up and she nudged her.

"You've got this," she said with a reassuring smile.

Cleo gave her a quick nod and blinked back the tears just as Nico walked over with a very pregnant woman. She plastered on a smile.

"Cleo, this is my sister, Mae. The birthday girl!"

Cleo held out her hand. "Nice to meet you, and happy birthday!"

"Thank you! Everything looks absolutely amazing. I've heard Nico and Kenny rave about you. I can't wait to try everything. In fact, I'm going to snag one of these right now."

Cleo watched as Mae picked up a mini strawberry cupcake. She popped the whole thing in her mouth. Her eyes opened wide as she looked from the cupcakes to Cleo.

"Okay. You're my new favorite person," said Mae.

"Told ya," said Nico.

Cleo laughed.

Mae turned to greet someone, but not before grabbing a cookie and calling over her shoulder, "I'll be back! Don't you go anywhere!"

"You're a hit," whispered Elle, as Cleo bit her lip to fight back the smile that wanted to explode onto her face.

Chapter 20

Kenny

She looked beautiful. Professional. Sexy. Delectable. More delectable than the desserts sitting in front of her on tiered trays. He'd tasted both, and as much as her pastries were delicious, she was even better tasting. It was difficult not to think about their night together when he saw her right in front of him. Hell, it'd been difficult not to think about it since it happened. But now, seeing her looking confident in a chef's coat, it was nearly impossible not to remember what was underneath. He craved her as much as his sweet tooth craved her creations.

He was careful not to get caught staring. He was careful when he entered the party to not look in her direction, not with the intention to hurt her, but because his heart might explode out of his chest. It took everything in him not to walk over and talk to her. She was probably avoiding him too, anyway. Why wouldn't she? After what he had done. How he had left her that morning.

Knowing he would be seeing her tonight, he took his time getting ready for the party. He had his suit finely pressed and had tried to wrangle his hair, which was always quite the task. When he had walked out of his bedroom, Nico eyed him surprised.

"Dang. I'm going to have to step it up." He looked down at his dress shirt and slacks, and went back to his bedroom to change into a suit. They drove separately to the party because Nico had to get there early to make sure everything was set up properly. He had invited Kenny along, but Kenny had declined. The less time alone with Cleo was probably better.

He took another long sip of his whiskey, finishing it. He looked down at his empty glass, and as if on cue, Justin walked up and handed him another. Kenny was thankful his best friend was in town to be here with him.

"Thanks," Kenny said, leaning against the wall. He snuck another glance in Cleo's direction.

"Why don't you go talk to her?"

Kenny shrugged. Justin still didn't know what had happened between the two of them.

"You're just going to stare at her all night?" asked Justin, looking from Kenny to Cleo.

"It's complicated."

"You like her. It sounds like she likes you. Seems easy."

"I think I screwed it up."

Justin raised his eyebrows as if waiting for Kenny to explain.

Kenny took a sip of his drink and sighed. "We slept together."

"What? When?" Justin choked on his drink.

"The night I left New York. I went straight to her house. I wasn't thinking."

"Sounds like you were thinking with something besides your brain. How was it?" Justin wiggled his eyebrows.

"Fucking amazing," whispered Kenny.

"Then what's the problem?"

"I left. I got scared and left. Well, I did have a meeting with coach that I couldn't miss, but I could have handled my exit better."

"Please tell me you called her after?"

Kenny shook his head.

"Texted?"

Kenny shook his head again.

"I left a note. Saying sorry and talk soon, or something like that. I haven't heard from her."

"Not surprising."

"Yeah, I know. But now you know why I can't just go over there. It's been a week, and nothing. It's over."

"I doubt that with how she's looking right at you." Justin gave him a smirk.

It took everything in Kenny not to look up and hopefully meet her gaze. Instead, he pushed off the wall and motioned toward the appetizer table.

"I'm starved. Let's eat."

He and Justin filled their plates with roasted vegetable skewers, goat cheese puffs with spicy red pepper jam, and bruschetta. Everything was delicious. Nico had really gone all out for his sister's party, with the help of her husband, Jonas. Kenny finished his plate and began mingling with the other guests at the party. After another drink, he started to feel a bit more comfortable and was actually having fun. He even felt brave enough to shoot a few more glances at Cleo, who was busy talking with guests who were gushing over her desserts.

She really was beautiful, and passionate about what she did. Kenny had never met anyone like her. Her dreams were big and her working toward them was impressive. Sexy. Most of the women he met nowadays were just into him for his job or his paycheck. They didn't have their own thing going on, which was why it never turned into anything serious. Well, at least one of the reasons.

Kenny had been shut off for so long that he couldn't even imagine any type of romance back in his life. There was room for it. Baseball took up a lot of his time, but not all of it. Some nights he would prefer being at home or out on a date, rather than partying with the team. Still, one-night stands were easier. There was no attachment. There were no expectations. There was no romance.

With Cleo, it was different. She was definitely a romance kind of girl, and he couldn't give her what she wanted. What she deserved. He found himself staring at her longer than he intended, thinking about what could be and what could not be. She must have felt his eyes on hers because she looked up and glanced around curiously, until her eyes landed on his. With their eyes locked, Kenny felt so much run through him all at once. He panicked and looked away quickly.

Just then, Jonas came to the center of the room and got everyone's attention. As he spoke, servers came around with trays of champagne, passing them out to the guests. Kenny noticed that Cleo had disappeared into the kitchen.

"I want to thank everyone for coming to celebrate my beautiful wife, Mae's, birthday."

Everyone clapped their hands as she hobbled over to her husband and linked her arm with his. He placed his hand gently on her growing belly and smiled down at her appreciatively.

"We have quite the adventure ahead, and I can't think of anyone else I would rather spend it with. I can't wait for our new life as a family to begin. Happy birthday, my love!" Jonas raised his glass and everyone followed suit.

Nico began singing happy birthday and everyone joined in, filling the room with song. Then there were gasps from the crowd as Cleo emerged from the kitchen with a four-tiered red velvet cake and dripping white frosting, with a large sparkler sitting at the top shooting bright sparks everywhere. Her smile was beaming as the crowd admired the cake she brought out.

She set the cake on a large, round table that had been moved to the center of the room. Mae looked at the cake in awe and gave Cleo a big hug, which took Cleo by surprise, but she hugged her back with a big smile. She pulled away and her assistant handed her the cake knife. Mae cut into the cake expertly and pulled away a large slice as a large explosion of sprinkles fell from the center of the cake, making the crowd gasp with delight.

Nico came up and stood next to Kenny.

"Wow. She really went all out. The sprinkles were a surprise to me."

"She's good. Really good." Kenny said in agreement.

"Thank you for finding her. Mae looks so happy."

"Happy to help."

Cleo and her assistant began plating the cake and handing it out to the party guests who were eager to get their hands on it. Kenny carefully observed everyone as they dipped their forks into the moist cake and brought it to their mouths. Every single one of them closed their eyes with satisfaction and began murmuring and eyeing Cleo, who had retreated back to the dessert table.

He watched as she and Elle talked quietly but excitedly as they overlooked the party. She was a total hit. The guests began flooding the dessert table and filling their plates with pastries and paying Cleo compliments.

"That was the best cake I have ever tasted."

"Where can I find your bakery?"

"Are you booked next month? I have a baby shower I need to plan."

"Do you have to-go boxes?"

He eavesdropped as she answered the questions happily. This was the push she needed. Kenny couldn't help but feel a small sense of pride in helping her in a small way. He wanted to help her more, and he was financially able to. With his job, there was definitely money to spare. The thought of lending her money as a business loan crossed his mind.

He didn't know her financial situation or what she made at the bar, but after tonight she would probably need a bigger space than her home kitchen to work out of. He could hire someone to help her find a space to rent, and she could work out of there until she was ready to open the doors as a bakery.

"You look deep in thought," said Nico, looking at him questioningly.

"Sorry. I'm here." He lifted his champagne glass and clinked it against Nico's.

"Cheers to an amazing party for Mae," said Kenny before taking a sip.

"Cheers!" said Nico enthusiastically.

Kenny pushed the thought of the business loan out of his head. Something about offering Cleo money just didn't sit right, especially since they no longer talked or had anything to do with each other. Even if he did offer, he doubted she would accept it.

He finished his champagne and he and Nico joined the rest of his team at the bar.

Chad ordered the team a round of drinks and held up his glass. "Cheers to Nico for finding his path in party planning. May he put this much effort into our next game."

The team laughed as Nico rolled his eyes. They clinked their glasses. Kenny couldn't help but notice Kev looking in Cleo's direction. He wasn't discreet about it as he leaned up against the bar sipping his drink and staring. It looked like he had some dark thoughts passing through his mind, which made Kenny uncomfortable.

Feeling protective, he stepped in front of Kev.

"What's so interesting?" asked Kenny, blocking his view.

"I'm just looking. That baker girl has a lot to look at." Kev peered past Kenny's shoulder, and Kenny swiftly stepped in front of him again.

"What the hell is your problem?" asked Kev, raising his voice.

"I just don't want you making anyone uncomfortable, especially the staff."

"Since when do you care about the staff? Or is it just someone in particular?" Kev stepped closer to Kenny as if challenging him.

Nico stepped between them. "Boys, boys, boys. We're at a party. For my sister. Let's not get into it here."

Kenny stood his ground, staring coldly at Kev, who took an unsure step back. He finished his drink and slunk away into the crowd. As he watched Kev disappear into the crowd in the opposite direction of the dessert table, Kenny felt like he could relax. That guy was such a creep. He didn't want him anywhere near Cleo.

"What was *that* about?" asked Nico.

"Nothing. Kev is just a total creep."

"Duh."

Kenny glanced to the dessert table, but Cleo was gone. He looked away disappointed. He couldn't help but beat himself up for not talking to her. The party was starting to wind down, and all they shared was one look. That one look was enough to knock the air out of him, but it still didn't provide any answers on where they stood.

Maybe it was better this way, especially since Kenny didn't know if he could give her what she wanted. His heart was torn between slipping out of the party undetected or finding her and taking her in his arms, if she'd let him. He stood there amidst the crowd and thought about his next move.

Chapter 21

Cleo

Once the birthday song was sung, a happy Mae blew out her ginormous sparkly candle. After Cleo cut and plated the cake for each guest but Kenny, she watched everyone dig into their cake with pride. They gave her the exact reaction she strived for whenever she baked anything, which somehow made her heart swell at the same time it broke.

The whole night she had snuck glances in Kenny's direction. She couldn't help it. It was as if he was a magnet. The fact that he was in a nice suit didn't help much. Out of all her sly stares, one locked with his. That one look tore her open. She felt yearning, lust, want, and need. Everything but love. Or so she convinced herself. And then it was gone. Interrupted by a speech and the reminder of how different their worlds were. How different their feelings were.

She couldn't bear being in the same room with him any longer.

"I'm heading to the kitchen," whispered Cleo as she started backing away from the cake table.

"I've got this." Elle gave her a convincing, but worried, look.

Cleo walked briskly away from the laughter and the clinking of glasses to the safety of the large kitchen. This was her happy place. She leaned against the cool counter and closed her eyes, soaking in the quiet and the absence of Kenny.

Still, she could feel him everywhere. Like static electricity buzzing off her skin. How could they be separated by one wall and still feel worlds apart? She gripped the counter tightly and shook her head. How could she have let herself fall for him? How could she have walked right into the role of a fool?

She knew as soon as he showed up that night at her house that it would be trouble. As much as she tried to talk herself out of the inevitable in the point-five seconds it took him to walk toward her, she still couldn't pull her lips away from his. Again, he was a magnet and nothing was going to be able to pull them apart. All the worries, what ifs, and fear she fought off in that one kiss, she just let herself fall.

It was one of the best nights of her life, but was it worth it? She had hoped tonight would give her answers. She had hoped he would be man enough to find her and explain everything. She had hoped she would be strong enough to demand answers if he couldn't. Turned out they were both weak.

But now was the time for Cleo to be strong. This party was just a reminder that she would never fit into his life or his heart. She wasn't rich and didn't wear cocktail dresses and didn't know a good wine from a boxed one. Looking around the room made her so much more aware of just who she was. A baker working her way up from the bottom to live an average, but happy life. She didn't need the frills or the parties or the large mansions.

She did fear that part of her needed Kenny, or at least wanted him more than she had ever wanted anybody. This scared her, and was just another reminder that she had to cut things off with this life. With him. With these people.

Yes, she'd lose out on opportunities. Her business cards had been cleared out. This was just what her business needed, but it wasn't worth the pain she felt. She couldn't risk seeing Kenny again at another party. No, she would have to start from scratch. She only had herself to blame.

Cleo sighed heavily and pushed herself from the counter with a confidence that she had to fake, even to herself, in order to make it through the end of the party. She began breaking down pastry boxes and washing the empty trays of frosting and leftover crumbs. The busywork was a good distraction from the party still going on just outside.

"How is it going in here?" asked Elle as she brought in some more empty dessert trays.

"Good. The boxes are all broken down. I'm just going to wash these." Cleo took the trays from Elle's arms.

"They cleared you out. The cake's almost gone, too. Who knew all these skinny women could eat so much cake?"

Cleo laughed as she turned on the sink. Elle leaned against the counter and looked at her.

"What?" asked Cleo, grabbing a scrub brush.

"Are you okay?"

"Yeah. Why wouldn't I be?"

"Oh, I don't know. It could be the very cute baseball player that's been looking at you all night, but is too stubborn to come over."

"He was not."

"Was too."

Cleo turned off the sink and began drying the trays on the counter.

"You know he sent his friend over to grab a plate of desserts?"

"Seriously?"

"Yes, as soon as you walked in the kitchen, that handsome CEO-type came over and loaded up a plate. I watched them devour everything."

Cleo was happy her desserts were a hit, but pissed that Kenny was too scared to come over himself.

"Well, I'm glad everything was a hit. You should probably get back out there. I'll finish up in here."

Elle pushed herself from the counter and gave Cleo a little salute before she disappeared back to the party.

Why was Kenny being so immature? He was acting like a scared little boy and Cleo could feel her sadness was starting to turn to anger. She took a deep breath and continued drying the trays. She was better off, anyway.

Someone walked into the kitchen. For a moment, she hoped it would be Kenny, but when she turned around, she felt a pit of dread in her stomach. It was Kev. The creep from the bar. She rolled her eyes and started placing the dessert trays back in the cabinets, ignoring him.

She could feel his eyes on her, making her uncomfortable as she stood on her tiptoes and her dress slid up slightly. She set the tray down quickly and pulled at her dress before turning around to face him.

"I'm just packing up in here. Do you need something?" Cleo crossed her arms.

"I was looking for something sweet. I heard you're just the girl." Kev leaned against the fridge wearing that awful smirk of his.

"Well, I'm fresh out. There might be some cake left. My assistant can help you out with that." Cleo waved toward the kitchen door.

"I don't need any more cake." He pushed himself up from the fridge and took a slow step toward her.

"Well, I'm not sure what I can do for you then."

"I think you do." Kev swirled his drink around before taking a sip. Cleo listened to the ice cubes clink in his glass. She suddenly felt very aware of every sound and every movement he made. She also suddenly felt very aware of how distant the party sounded. Her ears strained to hear if anyone was coming.

"I really need to get back to work."

"Always playing hard to get." Kev shook his head, amused, as he took another step toward her.

"I'm just here to work. I'm not interested in anything else." Cleo took a step backward.

"Just give me a chance."

Cleo took another step and her back hit the counter. There was nowhere else to go. She was trapped and looked at the doorway of the kitchen. She thought she should yell out, but she didn't want to make a scene. He was probably just drunk and running his mouth.

She gripped the counter behind her as he took another step toward her. He was slow in his movements, like a predator approaching his prey. Soon, his face was inches from hers. She could smell the vodka on his breath and it made her shudder. She tried to side-step him, but he put his hands over hers on the counter and held them down.

"Let me go," said Cleo sternly.

Kev ignored her and held her hands even tighter as he pressed his body against hers. She pulled her face away from his and went to cry out, but then his lips were on hers. She pressed her lips shut tightly and tried to move away, but he was crushing her under the weight of his body. There was nowhere to go.

Cleo then made a choice, and not an easy one. It took everything in her to act like she was enjoying it. He let his tongue part her lips and she pressed her body into his. She even let out a little moan to really sell it. He loosened his grip on her hands and moved his hands to her hair. Now was her chance. She grabbed a pan hanging behind her and slammed it into his head.

He stumbled backward, landing on the floor.

"You stupid bitch," he spat at her, but he stayed on the floor, holding his head.

She quickly ran around the kitchen island, grabbing her phone and bag and running down the hallway. She pushed past a few party guests, catching them off guard, but she didn't care. She found a bathroom and locked herself inside.

Her heart was pounding out of her chest and she felt like she was suffocating. She looked at herself in the mirror and saw a scared little girl looking back at her. She burst into tears. She was sick to her stomach. She could still taste him. The last thing she had wanted to do was kiss him, but she didn't know what else to do. She had to act weak in order to be strong.

She turned the sink on and cupped water in her hands, splashing it on her face and rinsing her mouth out. She continued until she was sure she couldn't taste the vodka or his tongue anymore. She dried her splotchy face and sat on the toilet. After a few deep breaths, she texted Elle:

I have to go. It's an emergency.

Cleo's phone immediately rang. It was Elle. Probably looking for an explanation. Probably worried by her lack of explanation. Cleo hit the ignore button. She was not ready to talk about what just happened. Her phone rang again and she ignored it.

Her phone dinged. It was a text from Elle:

Oh my god. Cleo. Where are you?

Cleo: *I'm leaving. I'll explain later.*

Elle: *Are you okay?*

Cleo: *I will be. I'll explain later. Can you finish cleaning up for me? I'll come get everything tomorrow or something.*

Elle: *Okay. Of course. Please call me later.*

Cleo: *I will.*

Cleo locked her phone and slid it into her bag. She heard a knock at the bathroom door and a surge of fear rushed through her. What if it was Kev? She didn't say anything. There was another knock and someone twisted the doorknob.

"Who is it?" she called out weakly.

"Er. I just need to use the bathroom," a woman called through the door.

Cleo felt a sigh of relief as she stood from the toilet and opened the door. A woman stood there looking at her curiously.

"Are you okay, dear?" The woman reached out her hand.

"I'm fine. Thank you." Cleo pushed past her and looked left and right. There was no sign of Kev. She clutched her purse and walked away from the sounds of the party. She wandered around quietly on edge until she finally found a side door that led out to a patio. She opened the door and ran to her car, fumbled with the keys, and finally unlocked it. Once inside, Cleo slammed the door, quickly locking it.

She turned the ignition and put it into drive, peeling out of the driveway without looking back. As she drove home, she blinked back tears.

Chapter 22

Kenny

Kenny scooped up his last bite of cake with his fork and savored it on his tongue before swallowing it. He looked over at Justin, who was licking his fork clean.

"Told you she was good." Kenny laughed.

"Better than good." Justin licked his fork again. "I still can't believe you made me go over there and get you a slice. I felt like I was in middle school again."

"I know. I know." Kenny felt embarrassed.

"She wasn't even there. That cute assistant was, though."

"I know. I don't know what's wrong with me."

"I do. You've caught feelings."

Kenny shook his head as he set his plate down at a nearby table.

"You're really stubborn, you know that?" Justin continued.

"I know."

"Like, she was right there." Justin waved toward the dessert table.

"I know," Kenny groaned.

"Where is she, anyway? She wouldn't be hard to miss in that pink coat," said Justin, looking around. The party was starting to wind down.

"I don't know. I haven't seen her in a while."

Kenny glanced at the dessert table and saw Cleo's assistant stacking plates and carrying them to the kitchen. Had she left? There was no way. Not with everyone asking for her info. This was her big break. He continued searching the room, but she was nowhere to be found.

He spotted Kev walking unsteadily from the kitchen area. He was holding a bag of ice to his head and muttering to himself. He must have had one too many and clocked his head on something. But then, a wave of nausea washed over Kenny and he didn't know why. He took a deep breath to settle his stomach.

Suddenly, he felt like a big coward for not talking to her. He had so many opportunities to set things right. He could have texted her or called her. He could have gone to the bar and visited her. He could have walked the ten feet to talk to her face-to-face tonight. Now he had missed his chance, and the full weight of it was hitting him.

Feeling a surge of courage, and slight panic, he walked over to the dessert table where Cleo's assistant was busy stacking plates. He cleared his throat nervously. Her assistant looked up with a smile that quickly disappeared when she saw him.

"Can I help you?" she asked curtly.

"Yeah. I was wondering where the head baker was?"

She ignored him and continued clearing the table.

"Er, I'm Kenny." He held out his hand.

"Elle." She shook his hand before briskly taking her hand back.

"So, can you tell me where your boss is?"

"Cleo."

"Hmm?"

"Her name is Cleo, but I think we both know that." Elle stacked a few trays and made her way to the kitchen.

Realizing this wasn't going to be easy, he followed her.

"Let me help you with that," said Kenny as he jogged to keep up with her, reaching for the stack of trays.

"I've got it."

They walked into the kitchen and Elle set the trays down on the counter. Kenny glanced around and realized Cleo wasn't there either. A stack of folded pastry boxes lay on the counter neatly, but her pink chef coat was thrown on the counter carelessly. Elle turned to leave the kitchen and go back to the party.

"Wait. Please," pleaded Kenny.

She turned to face him, shooting him a sharp look. She put her hands on her hips and raised her eyebrows questioningly.

"Where is she?" he asked softly.

"Cleo left," she said matter-of-factly.

"Wait, what?"

"Yeah." Elle shrugged.

Kenny couldn't believe she had left. He had missed his chance and now he was kicking himself. He tried to hide his disappointment, but failed miserably.

"That's too bad."

"Is it?" Elle said sarcastically.

Kenny was starting to wonder if Elle was merely Cleo's assistant or her good friend. Judging by her attitude and the lack of information she was providing, he assumed the latter. She probably knew everything. She probably hated him, and with good reason.

Ignoring his thoughts, he said, "Yeah. There are a few guests wanting her info for events."

"She's fresh out of business cards."

Kenny gave a solitary nod and chewed the inside of his cheek. They stood in silence for a minute. Clearly, this was going nowhere. He would have to find her himself.

"Okay. Well, thanks anyway."

He turned and walked out of the kitchen. He could have sworn he heard Elle mutter the word "asshole" under her breath, and he couldn't disagree with her. He walked back to the party and found Justin on his second slice of cake.

"She left." Kenny sighed.

"Well, it's not like you don't have her number. Or know where she works. Or know where she lives," said Justin sarcastically.

Kenny rolled his eyes, but his friend was right. He needed to step up to the plate. Something he knew how to do quite well in baseball, but not with the opposite sex. He decided he would talk to her in person. It was the right thing to do.

The next day, he spent hours working up the courage to go talk to her. He didn't want to show up at her house again. He didn't think he would be as welcome this time. Instead, he headed to Murphy's to see if she was working. He assumed she was because it was the weekend. He arrived at 4 p.m., just as the bar was opening for the night.

He pushed open the bar doors and looked around slowly as his eyes tried to adjust to the dim lighting. There were two men sitting at the bar who glanced at him and began whispering to themselves excitedly. He ignored them and looked behind the bar, but didn't see her. Maybe she was in the back. He saw Bridget behind the register and gave an awkward wave. She didn't look pleased to see him. That was weird. Maybe she didn't realize it was him. She was always so friendly when he and the team came in.

As he started to walk toward the bar, Bridget walked out from behind the counter and met him halfway. She crossed her arms and stood in front of him as if to block him.

"Kenny. You shouldn't be here," she said shortly.

"What?" Kenny was taken aback. She definitely knew him and wanted him out.

"She's not here."

"But I—"

"Look, Kenny. She's not here. It's probably best if you just leave her alone."

Kenny felt like he was having déjà vu. First, the icy encounter with Elle, now this with Bridget. What the hell was going on? Sure, he messed up, but he didn't think everyone knew about it or that he would be shunned like this. He shook his head in frustration before heading toward the door. He pulled open the doors and strode to his car.

In the driver's seat, he ran his hands through his hair and took a deep breath. He grabbed his phone and typed out a text:

Cleo. Can we talk?

He waited impatiently for a response. After ten minutes, he called her. It rang once before going to voicemail. He decided make the drive to her house. On the way there, he had a pit in his stomach. Something was wrong, and it was more than just him screwing up. He pressed his foot on the gas with the need to get to her quickly. He didn't care anymore if he was welcome or not. He had to see her. He had to find out what was going on. He had to fix it.

Kenny pulled into her driveway and looked up at her house for a moment before getting out. He remembered how differently he had felt the last time he showed up unannounced. There was anticipation and lust and another feeling he wouldn't admit. Now he was just filled with dread and guilt.

He couldn't tell if she was home or not. She still hadn't texted him back in the twenty minutes it took him to get there. He climbed out of his car and jogged up the sidewalk to the front door. He rang the doorbell and waited, tapping his foot anxiously. After a minute, he rang it again. He could have sworn he had heard the television on at first, but now it was silent. Maybe he had imagined it or maybe she really was ignoring him?

He pressed his forehead against the door and closed his eyes in defeat.

"Cleo, it's me. Please open up," he said through the door.

He waited a few more minutes, but no one came to the door. He was beginning to feel helpless. This was his only chance to see her for a while. He and the team were heading on the road early the next morning for a week.

He banged his fist on the door in frustration before walking back to his car. He peeled out of the driveway and headed home. His emotions were riding high with anger, frustration, and worry. When he walked into his condo, he threw his keys on the table roughly.

"You okay, man?" Nico looked at him curiously from the couch.

Kenny plopped down beside him and rubbed the sides of his face with his hands. "I messed up. Bad."

"What? How?"

Kenny finally came clean about everything with Cleo as Nico listened intently.

"I *knew* you two had a thing going on," said Nico, slapping his leg with his hand triumphantly.

"Yeah, but I screwed it all up. I was too scared at the party to talk to her, and now she is definitely ignoring me."

"Can you blame her?"

"No. I just want to talk to her. I'm worried about her."

"She did leave the party rather abruptly. Mae wanted to talk to her about hiring her for another event. I thought she would at least say goodbye."

"See? It's weird, right? She was so excited for the job and then she just disappeared."

"Hmm." Nico twisted his mouth as he thought about it. "I don't know, man. I *do* know that you need to get your head in the game, though. We have a long week ahead and Coach is already on you about missing practice. You're on his radar. So am I. Thanks to you."

"Ugh. I'm sorry, man. See? This is why I don't get involved with women." Kenny sat back and sunk into the couch frustratedly.

"No, this is why you don't screw up with women," Nico corrected him.

"True."

They spent the next hour vegging out on the couch watching an action movie. Nico grabbed a few beers from the fridge, and Kenny tried his best to get his mind off Cleo. He kept trying to push away the nagging feeling that something was really wrong. He knew Nico was right. He had to focus on baseball and the week ahead. There was no room for distractions.

The next morning, he woke up to the beeping of his alarm clock. It was 5 a.m. He groaned as he reached over and slammed the button to turn it off. He rubbed his eyes and let out a big yawn before remembering. Cleo. He reached for his phone eagerly in hopes she had texted him back, but there were no notifications. He rolled out of bed and grabbed his packed suitcase and duffle bag. He didn't care what he looked like or if he brushed his teeth or not. He just wanted to get on the road.

Maybe the distance would help him make the sinking feeling disappear. He could just focus on the game, practice, and getting from place to place. It's what he should do. He was in hot water with his coach. It seemed like he was in hot water with everyone. Maybe when he got back home, Cleo would have cooled down and she would be ready to talk to him. He could only hope.

Chapter 23

Cleo

Cleo listened from the couch to the sound of Kenny's car pulling out of the driveway. When she was sure he was gone, she let out the breath she was holding and shut her eyes tightly, trying to fight back the tears that were burning. She was not expecting him to show up today and it was completely throwing her.

When she had first heard the doorbell ring, she was in the middle of mindlessly watching whatever was on TV, trying to get her mind off yesterday. It had startled her. It had also scared her. What if it was Kev? How did he find her? She sat on the couch shaking and trying hard to listen for clues of who it might be.

After another knock, she finally heard Kenny's voice through the door. He sounded so sad. So pleading. So helpless. It almost made her stand up and fling open the door. For a fleeting moment she wanted him to wrap his arms around her and make her feel safe. But then she remembered what had happened between them.

He had left her that morning without saying another word to her. He had ignored her at the party when she was right in front of him. She thought about how things might have ended so differently if he would have just talked to her or made it known that there was something between them. Maybe if he did, Kev wouldn't have done such an awful thing.

Or maybe it wouldn't have mattered, but at least her heart would have felt safer with him if he had talked to her or apologized for leaving things the way they were.

So instead of letting him in, she kept him shut out. She clutched a blanket tightly around her and stayed hidden by the back of the couch, holding her breath. It felt like an eternity before he finally got back in his car.

She rolled onto her back and stared tiredly at the ceiling. She had barely slept last night. Visions of Kev's menacing smirk, his hands crushing hers, and his lips on her lingered in her head. It all made her sick. She fought off nausea all night. So much so that she tossed and turned or ran to the bathroom thinking she was going to be sick.

That morning, she felt like she had been hit by a truck. Her hands were sore from where Kev had squeezed them against the countertop, as if she needed another reminder of what had happened. She knew she had to call Elle and let her know she was okay. With the way she was feeling, it was probably a good idea to ask Bridget for the night off.

When she turned her phone on there were several missed calls from Elle, and a missed call and text from Kenny. She quickly opened it.

Cleo. Can we talk?

She shook her head and closed out of the text. She typed out a quick text to Elle:

I'm okay. I'll explain everything later. Thank you for finishing up last night. I owe you.

She wasn't ready to explain what had happened yet. Even to her best friend. She texted Bridget next:

I'm so sorry to do this, but I'm not feeling very well. Do you think someone can cover my shift tonight?

She felt bad for taking another night off work after Bridget had given her time off for last night's party. The last place she wanted to go was the bar tonight. She didn't want to be anywhere that Kev could just show up. She didn't want to be anywhere the team could show up. She wanted nothing to do with those people. Still, she knew she couldn't avoid her job forever. She just needed one more day.

Her phone dinged. It was Bridget:

Oh no! Don't worry about it. Just focus on feeling better.

Cleo smiled wanly before turning her phone back off. She settled back into the couch and turned the TV up. She had no plans of leaving her safe little cocoon until tomorrow. Tomorrow, she would face her life again.

The next day, she woke up around noon. She was happy for a good night's sleep and felt caught up from the night before. She rose from the couch as afternoon light poured in and warmed her skin. In the kitchen, she made herself a hot cup of coffee and sat at the kitchen table. She looked around her favorite spot in the house at all the mixing bowls and recipe books. She felt a glimmer of happiness.

She loved baking and still dreamt of opening her own bakery. Although that dream seemed even further now that she had decided to wash her hands of everyone at the party. Everyone in that world. She knew she was closing the door on several opportunities and that she would have to basically start from scratch again, but it was the right thing to do. Whatever happened with Kenny was too complicated, and what happened with Kev was too dangerous.

She took a sip of coffee and began scribbling ideas in a notebook, including new cafés she hadn't applied at yet. It was nice to keep her brain busy. When she was finished, she powered up her phone and texted Bridget:

I'm feeling much better. I'll be in tonight. Can we talk before my shift starts?

Bridget: *I'm so glad to hear that. Of course we can. I'll see you in a few hours.*

Cleo felt thankful for her positive relationship with her boss. She knew she was very lucky to have Bridget, especially since she would probably be working there longer than she had expected to save up for her dream.

The rest of the day, Cleo took it slow. She baked an olive oil cake just because. Baking was her therapy. After she enjoyed a slice with some hot tea, she took a long, hot shower. She actually didn't think of Kenny. At least not as much. Then she quickly got ready for work in her usual jeans and T-shirt. She didn't put in any extra effort. After the party, she felt silly for even trying so hard for someone who barely tried at all.

She pulled into the rear parking lot of Murphy's just after three. She entered the back door and waved hello to the cooks in the kitchen before pushing open the swinging doors to the bar. It wasn't open yet. Bridget sat at the bar sipping on an iced coffee.

"Hey, Cleo. I'm so glad you're feeling better. We've missed you the past few days."

"I know. I'm sorry for all the time off."

Bridget waved at her like it was no big deal. "Don't sweat it. You're my hardest worker. You need a break every now and again."

Cleo took a seat next to her.

"So, what did you want to talk about?" Bridget placed her hands in her lap and tapped her fingers nervously.

Cleo could sense that maybe Bridget thought she was quitting, so she wanted to reassure her.

"I'm not quitting."

"Oh, thank God."

Cleo laughed.

"I'm not ready to lose you yet."

"You're not, but I do have something to talk to you about."

Bridget nodded at her intently.

"Something happened at the party two nights ago. Something bad." Cleo shifted in her seat.

"What happened?" Bridget leaned in.

"One of the players on the team became forceful with me."

"Oh, my God, Cleo. Where? How? Who?"

"I was in the kitchen packing up, and that guy Kev… you know the one who was giving me a hard time that one night here?"

"Mhmm."

"He cornered me and pushed me up against the counter, forcing himself on me."

"Cleo! Did you call the police?"

"No, no. He just kissed me and then I hit him in the head with a frying pan."

"You need to tell someone."

"I'm telling you. He's a professional athlete. You know no one would believe me."

230

"I believe you. I don't care if anyone else doesn't. That guy deserves to pay for what he did to you."

"I just want to forget it happened." Cleo leaned back against her barstool.

"You should go home." Bridget laid her hand gently on Cleo's arm.

"No. I want to be here. I need to keep busy."

Bridget eyed her hesitantly before giving in. "Okay. If you say so. At least the team is on the road, so we won't have any problems tonight."

"Thank you, Bridget." Cleo hugged her.

Once the bar opened, it was a pretty slow night, but Cleo still kept busy with unboxing and shelving new bottles of liquor that had just been delivered. Bridget handled most of the customers, which Cleo was grateful for. She wasn't in the mood for much small talk. Bridget didn't put the game on any of the TVs. It was her way of boycotting, much to some of the customers' dismay.

After a few hours, Bridget came back into the kitchen to find Cleo.

"There's someone here to see you. A woman. A very pregnant woman."

Cleo let out a sigh. She could only think of one person.

"Thanks." She wiped her hand on a dishrag before heading out into the bar.

Mae sat uncomfortably on a barstool and waved eagerly at Cleo when she saw her.

"Hi, Cleo! Nico said I could find you here."

"What can I help you with? I'm guessing you're not here for a drink."

Mae let out a laugh. "No, no. I wish. Any day now, little one." She tapped on her belly gently.

"I was actually here to see if you could cater another event. I wasn't able to talk to you after the party. It was such a hit. Everyone just loved the dessert. And that cake! I've been dreaming of it."

Cleo shifted her feet uncomfortably. Mae was so nice and this was her big break being dangled right in front of her, but she had to hold her ground.

"I'm sorry. I can't."

"But I didn't even tell you when the party was."

"I don't want to do business with you."

Mae looked taken aback.

"Oh. I… I'm sorry to hear that. May I ask why?"

This was harder than she thought. Cleo looked around for Bridget as backup.

She immediately strode over. "Is there a problem here?"

"Oh no. I hope not. I was just hoping to hire Cleo again for another party. She's such a wonderful baker."

"I don't think she's interested. I think it's best if you leave."

It looked as if Mae might cry, which Cleo couldn't bear to look at, so she looked down at her feet. Mae struggled to push off the barstool, but eventually got down and grabbed her purse. She looked at Cleo sadly before waddling slowly out of the bar.

"You okay?" asked Bridget.

"Yes. I just feel so bad. She's so nice and she didn't do anything wrong. It's not her fault Kev did what he did."

"No, but you don't need to be associated with them. The further you distance yourself, the better. In fact, Kev is no longer welcome here. Neither is the team."

"But, Bridget. They bring in so much money, not to mention customers."

Bridget held her hand up. "I don't care. We're a family. We'll be fine without them."

Cleo looked at Bridget, who seemed so confident in her decision.

"I can't let you do that. This bar means too much to me, you, and your dad. I'll quit."

"No, you can't."

"I just did."

Cleo gave Bridget a tear-filled hug before walking out of the bar. She knew none of this was her fault, but she couldn't help but blame herself. She numbly got in her car and drove home. She had a lot to figure out.

Chapter 24

Kenny

As much as Kenny had wished his time on the road would get his mind off Cleo, she kept eating away at his thoughts. Despite his head being elsewhere, he played well. The team won every away game, which raised everyone's spirits. Even Kenny's. At least a little.

They had done the usual celebrating at the popular bars and clubs, but Kenny's heart just wasn't in it. He went through the motions, but just wanted to be back at the hotel. His teammates gave him a hard time at first, but then they just backed off and left him alone.

On the bus ride to the airport, Kenny opened his unanswered texts to Cleo. He had texted her a few times:

It's me again. I just want to talk.

I'm worried about you. Please text me back.

Are you there?

All of his texts remained unanswered. He sighed as he clicked his phone to lock and put it back in his pocket.

"You okay?" asked Nico, eyeing him from the seat next to his.

"Cleo hasn't texted me back all week."

"Yikes. The silent treatment."

"I just want to make sure she's okay. It still doesn't make sense that she just ditched the party like that."

"Yeah, it's pretty weird. She was really looking forward to the party and hopefully getting clientele."

"Has Mae said anything?"

Nico shook his head. "Other than her loving everything, no, nothing. I even called Jonas. Seeing how off you've been this week I thought having some answers would help you out, but he didn't know what happened. He just said everyone was raving about her. They wanted to hire her for another event, actually."

"Really? That's great."

"Yeah, but she hasn't returned their emails or calls."

"She can't be *that* mad at me that she would pass up on an opportunity like that."

"I don't know, man. Women are beautiful, but confusing creatures." Nico shrugged.

Kenny nodded as he laid his head back against the seat. Why was Cleo being like this? Sure, he had messed up. She didn't have to forgive him or talk to him, but to hear that she was giving the silent treatment to the team's owners was a mistake. This was her big break and she was throwing it away because of a guy?

Granted, he was a stupid guy, but still. It didn't make sense.

He remembered being in the kitchen with her that first afternoon together, seeing her in her element as she moved expertly through the kitchen. He remembered her smile as she flicked through her recipe books. He remembered her biting her lip in concentration as she used her measuring cups to pour in the flour and the sugar.

Those lips. Suddenly flashbacks of their night together hit him hard. Her soft lips against his, on his neck, on his chest. It was one of the best nights of his life. How could he have walked away from her? This smart, passionate woman. He couldn't let this go. He had to make it right with her, or at least figure out what happened at the party for her to give up. There had to be more to the story.

The flight home dragged on, but the team finally made it back to Boston at around 11 p.m. He tried texting Cleo again:

I'm back in Boston. I would love to talk. Please, Cleo.

When he got back to his condo, he unpacked, showered, and lay down on his bed. He started getting drowsy and gave up on waiting for a response from her.

The next morning, he woke up to no notifications. His frustration was growing. He went on a long run to clear his head.

When he got back to the condo, he heard people talking in the dining room. He peeked his head in and saw Nico, Mae, and Jonas eating breakfast.

"Hey, Kenny! We brought over some bagels. Do you want one?" asked Mae, holding up a brown paper bag.

"Sure. Thanks. Hey, boss."

"I'm just Jonas today."

Kenny took a seat at the table and grabbed an everything bagel from the bag, spreading cream cheese with a butter knife. He took a bite and listened to Mae talk about pregnancy and as the others took guesses as to when the baby would be here.

"You know, I was really hoping to order some more desserts from that girl, Cleo. You know, while I can afford to keep eating anything and everything." Mae laughed.

Jonas patted Mae's belly affectionately.

"It's too bad. I even had another event for her to cater, but she turned me down."

"Wait, you talked to her?" Kenny interjected.

"Mhmm. She wasn't returning my calls or emails after the party, so I went to that bar she works at."

"Was she there?"

"Yes, but she didn't want the job. She also didn't seem like she wanted anything to do with me." Mae frowned sadly.

"Really?" asked Kenny, surprised.

"Yeah, her boss actually kicked Mae out of the bar," said Jonas, with irritation in his voice. "Can you imagine kicking a nice, pregnant woman out? I have half a mind to go down there and chew them both out."

Mae laid a hand gently on Jonas's arm. "Now, now. There had to be a good reason."

"Like what?" Jonas raised an eyebrow.

"Something must have happened at that party," said Nico.

"All I can think of is…" started Mae.

"What?" asked Kenny.

"Maybe someone tried something. Maybe one of the players. It's the only thing I can think of that makes sense," said Mae thoughtfully.

Kenny felt his heart drop. Why hadn't he thought of that? But who was it? He thought back to the party and Kev holding ice to his head. Of course. It had to be him. He had been eyeing Cleo that night, and it wouldn't be the first time he had tried something with her.

Kenny clenched his fists under the table as he felt heat rise to his face. He could just see Kev making a move on Cleo. Overpowering her. It made him sick to his stomach.

"It was Kev," said Kenny suddenly.

"Wait, what? You knew?" asked Nico.

"I saw him at the party looking at Cleo with foul intentions."

"Let's not jump to conclusions," said Jonas, putting his hands up.

"No, I think Kenny might be right. Kev is a total creep. You should hear the things he says in the locker room, even about Mae," Nico said.

Mae held her hands up to her mouth in surprise. Jonas frowned.

"That's unfortunate to hear, but we can't take action unless we're sure," said Jonas seriously.

Kenny stood suddenly from the table. He couldn't sit there any longer trying to be diplomatic. Rage was pulsing through his veins. He had to find Kev. Now.

"Whoa. Where are you going?" asked Nico.

"I'm going to find him," said Kenny, turning to leave.

"Don't do anything you might regret," Nico called after him.

Kenny grabbed his keys from the entryway table and impatiently pushed the button for the elevator. While he waited, he called Kev. It went straight to voicemail. Kenny rode down to the parking garage, thinking of all the places Kev might be. He drove to his condo, but he wasn't there. He drove to the stadium, but he wasn't there. It was too early for him to be at the bar, and from the sounds of it, none of them were welcome there anymore. He drove to the team's gym as his last resort.

Kenny jogged up the stairs and peered through the large glass windows of the gym. He spotted Kev doing chest presses. His trainer was there talking him through his reps. Kenny pushed through the doors and strode over.

"Can you give us a minute?" he asked the trainer.

"Uh…sure." The trainer eyed Kenny and Kev warily before walking away.

"Why are you interrupting my training session?" asked Kev as he slid out from under the barbell and sat with his arms crossed on the bench.

"I just have some questions."

"Like what?" asked Kev, uninterested.

"Like what happened at Mae's party."

"I don't know what you're talking about." Kev stood up and grabbed his water bottle, taking a sip.

"I saw you. You were walking out of the kitchen with ice against the side of your head. Now that I think of it, you've had a pretty good-sized knot for the past week."

"I fell." Kev shrugged.

"You fell?" Kenny wasn't convinced.

"Yeah, I drank a little too much."

"That's nothing new."

"Why do you care so much?" Kev asked.

"Because I think something else happened at that party."

"You think I'm lying."

"I know you are." Kenny took a step closer and glared at him.

"Look, whatever that girl told you, she was lying. *She* wanted it." Kenny put his hands up.

"What girl?" Kenny wanted to hear him say it.

"The fat baker chick."

"Her name is Cleo." Kenny shoved Kev back, causing him to stumble over the bench.

"What the hell is your problem?" Kev yelled as he tried to right himself.

"What did you do to her?" Kenny towered over him.

"Nothing she didn't want," Kev sneered.

Kenny held his fists at his sides, cracking his knuckles and trying to keep it together.

"Oh wait. Was she yours? Lucky guy. She tasted so good," said Kev, licking his lips.

Kenny couldn't keep it in anymore. He raised his fist and slammed it into Kev's eye. He lifted it again and landed another blow across his nose. He raised another fist and landed it again.

Kev yelled out and his trainer came running out of the locker room.

"Hey! Stop! Get off!" He grabbed Kenny and pulled him off. He started dragging him away while he called security from his phone.

Kev stayed on the ground, but propped himself on his elbows shakily.

"I'll have you kicked off the team for this!" yelled Kev.

"I'll have you kicked off for assault," Kenny spat at him.

Just then, two security guards grabbed Kenny and pulled him out of the gym, while the trainer tended to Kev, who was bleeding from the nose and mouth. They dragged Kenny down the hallway. Just then, Nico and Jonas came out of a nearby elevator, looking around frantically.

"Sir. There's been an altercation in the gym," said one of the security guards to Jonas.

"You can let him go, gentlemen. Kenny, I trust you can get it together," said Jonas calmly.

"Yes, sir," said Kenny.

The security guards let him go reluctantly.

"That will be all." Jonas nodded toward the security office, and they walked slowly away.

"What the hell were you thinking?" asked Nico.

"I wasn't. But Kev admitted it. He definitely tried something on Cleo."

"Where is he now?" asked Jonas.

"In the gym." Kenny motioned down the hallway before clutching his right hand. It was red and sore.

"I'll get you some ice for that." Nico eyed his hand.

"Thanks."

As Nico walked away, Kenny turned to Jonas. "I'm sorry, sir. I know that violence is not an option on the team."

"No, no it's not. There will be consequences." Jonas shook his head ruefully.

Kenny looked down at his feet. He gulped as he wondered what would happen next. He would probably be kicked off the team, but it was worth it to take up for Cleo. That creep deserved what he got. He waited quietly for Jonas to say something.

"Sexual assault is never acceptable," said Jonas, putting a hand on Kenny's shoulder. "Kev is off the team. This is a warning for you, though. Next time, talk to me and keep your fists out of it."

"Yes, sir." Kenny watched as Jonas walked down the hallway to the gym.

He breathed a sigh of relief. Nico handed him a bag of ice, which he laid carefully on his hand. He grimaced from the pain.

"Let's go home," said Nico, patting him on the back.

Chapter 25

Cleo

Cleo stood at her kitchen counter, mindlessly whisking brownie batter in a mixing bowl. Since she had unexpectedly quit the bar, she went back to the one thing she knew: Baking. Her heart was broken from leaving Bridget hanging, but it was a small price to pay. In the end, the bar needed the team. She knew Kev wouldn't be allowed back, but the bar needn't suffer because of her.

Everyone at Murphy's had become Cleo's family. The other bartenders. The cooks. Bridget. Especially Bridget, who had so much on her shoulders since taking it over for her father. The bar was his pride and joy, and now hers. She didn't want to see a sick man sad when his business dipped. It wouldn't be right. Even though Bridget said they would make it work, Cleo could see the trickle of doubt on her face.

Bridget had been calling and calling, but Cleo ignored the calls. Eventually, she knew she would have to answer and tell her she was serious about quitting. She just needed to get her wits and strength about her to actually stay firm in her decision. She had to tell her she was moving back to Indiana. Giving up and going back to the safety of home seemed like her only choice. She had no job and her dream of opening a bakery seemed further away than ever.

Just then, her phone buzzed. It was a text from Kenny. Again. She glanced at the notification on her screen:

Please answer me, Cleo.

She stopped whisking and hung her head, allowing the tears she had been holding back to fall freely. She had been ignoring him, too. He had called and texted. She knew he was worried about her and wanted to make things right. She could tell from his messages, but she just couldn't bring herself to talk to him.

The truth was, she felt like a failure and she was embarrassed. She also felt empty inside since Kev had forced himself onto her. He had taken her power away. She hadn't talked to anyone about that part because she felt a mixture of fear and stupidity for letting him do that to her. Not that she had much of a choice. She hadn't even told Elle the truth. As much as her best friend pried, Cleo had lied and said it was too painful to see Kenny at the party, and that's why she left so suddenly. She didn't know why she couldn't open up about it. Deep down, she knew what Kev did to her wasn't her fault, but she still felt like a fool.

Just then, she heard a knock at her door, startling her. She wasn't expecting anyone. Cleo wiped her tears away with the back of her hand before walking slowly and quietly to the living room. She didn't want anyone to know she was home. Carefully, she peered through the window and saw a car she didn't recognize in the driveway. A nice one. For a moment, she felt the familiar fear rise inside her thinking it was Kev, but then she heard a woman's voice through the door.

"Cleo. It's me, Mae. Please open up."

Cleo let out a slow breath of relief that it wasn't who she feared. She hesitated, though. She had told Mae to stay away. Why was she here? How did she know where she lived? Cleo reluctantly unlocked the door as she wondered when this woman would get the hint. She opened the door slightly and poked her head out. Mae was standing there, and to her surprise, Cleo saw her husband, Jonas, standing there too.

"I really wish you would leave me alone," said Cleo, shaking her head.

"I know, and we will after this. I promise. But…" Mae looked at Jonas for support.

"We need to talk to you," said Jonas, giving her a reassuring nod. "Can we please come in?"

Cleo sighed and stepped back, pushing the door open and allowing them space to enter. Mae waddled past her and Jonas followed behind with his hand gently placed on his wife's back. Cleo motioned for them to sit down on the couch. Mae eased herself down with Jonas's help before he took the seat beside her. Cleo took a seat across from them in her favorite armchair. She looked at them sternly.

"Look, I already told you that I have no interest in working for you or for anyone else you might know."

"That's not why we're here," said Jonas.

"Then why *are* you here?" Cleo looked between them, confused.

Mae reached for Jonas's hand and held it tightly before looking at Cleo with sadness in her eyes.

"We heard what happened at the party."

"What did you hear?" Cleo couldn't believe what she was hearing. Did they know?

"What Kev did to you," said Mae softly.

Cleo's mouth opened slightly. This was the last thing she was expecting. "What? How did you find out?"

"It was Kenny, actually."

Cleo felt her heart speed up just hearing his name. "Kenny?" she asked, confused.

"He had his suspicions. Poor guy was really worked up about it, according to my brother. He hasn't been himself lately," said Mae.

"Oh." Cleo fiddled with her thumbs. Kenny knew. No wonder he was trying to get hold of her so insistently. And he knew her mouth had been interlocked with Kev's. Involuntarily, of course. It made her shudder. She sat in silence as she waited for Mae to continue.

"Kenny went and found Kev as soon as he put everything together."

"And?"

"Let's just say he eventually got the truth out of Kev."

"In a way I don't condone," interjected Jonas.

"But it was very valiant," said Mae, nodding.

"What do you mean?" asked Cleo.

"Let's just say Kev has a broken nose and a black eye," said Mae, almost proudly.

Cleo gasped and raised a hand to her mouth in surprise. He had fought Kev? For her? She suddenly felt very worried for Kenny, especially knowing how Kev could be.

"Is Kenny…" she started.

"He's fine," said Mae, finishing her question with reassurance. Suddenly, a knowing look crossed over Mae's face as she gave Cleo a small smile. She knew there was more to the story between her and Kenny. Cleo looked away shyly, as she felt her cheeks turning red.

"I want you to know we have a policy against violence," said Jonas seriously.

Cleo shot him a worried look. Had Kenny been kicked off the team? For her? Did he just ruin his dreams?

As if reading her mind, Jonas continued, "Kenny is still on the team, but he is benched for the next few games and there was a heavy fine he had to pay."

Cleo bit her lip nervously. He was in trouble, but he was still on the team.

Jonas continued, "But more importantly, Kev is off the team. As much as we don't condone violence, sexual assault is a non-negotiable."

"Wait, really?" she asked softly.

"Of course. I've contacted every owner in the business and let them know of his transgressions. He won't play again."

Cleo felt her eyes beginning to tear up. They believed her, and they did something about it. She wanted to rush over and hug them, but she remained quiet in the comfort of her armchair. Her thoughts were swirling around her head as she tried to grapple with what they were telling her.

"I want to apologize for the actions of one of my players. He does not reflect who we are as a team or an organization," said Jonas, sitting straighter. Cleo could tell he was an honest businessman. She felt she could trust him, which was hard for her to do, given recent events.

Mae pulled herself from the couch and walked over to Cleo. With some effort, she knelt down next to the armchair. She took Cleo's hands gently and gave them a squeeze.

"I am so sorry that happened to you, and at one of my parties. I just can't even bear the thought of it," she said.

Cleo nodded shakily and looked down at Mae, whose eyes were watering.

"I can't even imagine what you've been going through. I know this is a lot to think about, and I don't want to put any more stress on you. But if you want to press charges, please know that you have our full support. I will be your witness."

This was suddenly so overwhelming. Cleo shut her eyes. When she did, she saw Kev's face against hers. Felt his tongue down her throat. Then she imagined Kenny confronting him. She wondered if he was hurt at all. Then she thought of seeing Kev's face again in court, staring at her with his uncomfortable, piercing gaze. She felt short of breath. It was all too much.

"I'm fine," she blurted out, pulling her hands away and recoiling from Mae.

Mae looked at her with surprise.

"I'm actually moving back to Indiana. Away from all of this."

"Cleo," Mae started. She looked hurt.

"Look, I appreciate what you've done for me, but I'm going to have to ask you to leave. Please."

Jonas stood slowly from the couch and walked over to help Mae to her feet.

"Come on, honey. Let's give her some time to process." He led Mae to the door.

Before opening the door, he turned and said, "Please let us know what you decide about pressing charges. We stand with you no matter what."

He opened the door and led Mae out, closing it behind them. Cleo was alone again. She hugged her knees to her chest and replayed everything that had just happened. Kev had paid for what he did. He had been kicked off the team. These people she wanted nothing to do with had gone up to bat for her, without even hearing her side of the story. She shook her head before burying her head into her knees.

Kenny had figured it out. He had been so worried about her that he had put it all together. For a moment, she felt guilty for ignoring him. He had fought for her and paid the price, but at least he was still on the team. She was happy he hadn't been punished too harshly. She would never forgive herself if he lost out on his dreams. If one of them had to give up on their dreams, she was glad it was her. Not him.

She had the urge to text him or call him. She wanted to hear his voice. She wanted to know if he was okay. More so, she wanted him to wrap his arms around her and erase the memories of Kev's hands on her. She wanted to feel his lips on hers and wipe away the thought of Kev's gruffness. She wanted him to lie over her like a blanket and make everything okay. She thought she would never want to be touched again by a man, but suddenly the thought of Kenny holding her was the only thing she wanted.

But he had done enough for her, and she had messed up his life enough in the few months of knowing each other. It was better to fight her urges and keep her distance. Everything was too complicated. It was complicated even before the party. It was time to move on.

At least she could move back to Indiana knowing that Kev got what he deserved, and she had a small amount of justice for what he did to her. She did feel sad thinking of leaving Boston and everything behind. Her job. Her best friend. Her dream of owning a bakery in the big city. Kenny, the first guy who had made her feel something. Especially now that she knew she had the support of everyone, it made it that much harder. But she had made up her mind.

Chapter 26

Kenny

"Wait. She's moving?" asked Kenny, raising his voice.

Jonas put his hands up, mocking defense. "Don't shoot the messenger."

"I can't believe it." Kenny shook his head slowly as he processed this new information.

Cleo was moving. She was leaving Boston and heading back to Indiana. With all that had happened, Kenny still hadn't gotten through to her. She never texted him back. She never called him back. He knew he would not be welcomed at the bar. The small hope he had left was starting to diminish even more now that he knew she was leaving. He didn't know when, which was troublesome.

"Mae and I tried to talk to her. Let her know we're on her side," explained Jonas.

"And? How was she?"

"The girl was a mess. As she should be. Mae cried on the way home because she felt so bad. Her pregnancy hormones aren't helping either."

Kenny ran his hands through his hair as he thought about Cleo. She must be so scared after what Kev did to her. He had half a mind to beat his ass again, but it wouldn't accomplish anything other than satisfy his anger that kept bubbling to the surface. Kev would never play ball again, at least not professionally. He got what he deserved.

Still, hearing how Cleo was struggling didn't make Kenny feel any better. He tried his best to push away the images of what Kev did to her at the party, but his imagination got the better of him. It made him sick to his stomach. If this was how he felt, he couldn't imagine how she felt. Being hurt by him, being assaulted by Kev, and not being able to get her baking business off the ground. It was a lot for one person. It made sense that she wanted to go back to the comfort of home and try to heal.

"I know you're worried about her. Why don't you talk to her?" asked Jonas.

"I've tried. Believe me. She won't text me back."

"Then go over there and see her."

"Yeah, I should. I just don't want to scare her."

Jonas studied him for a moment. "Mae told me she sensed something was going on between you."

"Really?" asked Kenny, surprised.

"She said it was something in the way Cleo asked about you. She was worried about you after she heard what happened between you and

Kev. Mae picked up on a vibe that you two were more than friendly."

Kenny shifted in his seat. He felt a little uncomfortable talking about his love life with his boss, but after what he did for Cleo, he was starting to feel more like a friend.

"Mae was right."

Jonas raised his eyebrows, inviting Kenny to tell him more.

"It started off friendly, but then it turned into more. Then, of course, I had to go and screw it up. Now everything is so complicated."

Jonas waited a moment before speaking.

"You know…Mae and I didn't have the easiest start either. She will be the first to tell you how badly I messed up."

"Really?" Kenny didn't know about their history, so this was news to him. They seemed like such a solid couple. So in love.

"Yeah. Twice, actually. But she gave me another chance, and I count my blessings every single day. She is my person, and now she's having our baby. We couldn't be happier."

Kenny looked down at his lap, processing what Jonas was saying.

"Maybe Cleo is *your* person. You won't know if you don't try," Jonas continued. He nudged Kenny with his shoulder.

Kenny gave him a small smile. "Yeah. Maybe you're right."

Jonas cleared his throat and sat up a little taller. "Now, the reason I'm here is not to give relationship advice."

"Right," laughed Kenny.

"Time to pay up. As much as Kev deserved what he got, we still have to abide by the rules."

Kenny stood up from the couch and walked to the entryway table of his condo. He opened a drawer and pulled out a checkbook. Jonas was here to collect the fine for breaking the "no violence" policy. Regardless, Kenny felt thankful that he had not lost his place on the team. Sure, he had to sit out for a few games, and he had a hefty fine to pay, but it was worth it.

He sat down next to Jonas and scribbled the amount on the check. He signed it before handing it to Jonas.

"I wanted to say thank you again for not cracking down harder on me," said Kenny.

"Let's just not have it happen again."

"Yes, sir."

Jonas stood from the couch, and Kenny walked him to the elevators.

"Don't forget what I said," said Jonas before the doors closed.

Kenny smiled to himself. Even though this seemed like an impossible situation with Cleo, Jonas had made him feel better. His boss was actually a big softie. Maybe he was right. Maybe

Cleo was his person. Since meeting her, despite the messiness, he had a lingering feeling that she was different from anyone else. There was something special there.

Kenny glanced at his phone for the time. It was just after seven. It was Friday, which meant she was probably working at the bar tonight. He knew she was too good of a person to just leave town and leave the bar empty-handed. There was no point in going over there. He probably wouldn't be allowed in. If they kicked out a very pregnant Mae, there was no way he was getting in. Despite this, he did feel better that at least she would be protected from Kev. As nice as Bridget was, she seemed like a mama bear. He would have to wait until she was off.

He had several hours to wait, so Kenny made an easy dinner and sat at the kitchen table to eat. He had just picked up his fork when Nico walked in.

"Something smells good." He sniffed the air and looked around curiously.

"I made spaghetti." Kenny shoveled a forkful in his mouth.

"*You* cooked?" Nico walked over and lifted the lid of the pot, looking inside.

"Help yourself," said Kenny around a mouthful.

Nico grabbed a bowl and filled it to the top. He came and sat next to Kenny, then took a big bite and gave Kenny an impressed look. "This is actually good."

"You can't really mess up spaghetti."

"Yeah, you can. Trust me."

Kenny laughed.

Nico lifted his fork to his mouth. "So, what's up? You're cooking and staying in on a Friday night?"

"I'm just trying to kill time. Distract myself. I'm going to go see Cleo later."

"Mmmm." Nico looked at him skeptically.

"Jonas told me she's moving back to Indiana," Kenny admitted.

"And you're going to try and stop her…?"

"I'm going to try."

"Good. I like Cleo," said Nico certainly.

Kenny smiled to himself before taking another bite. He finished his bowl and placed it in the kitchen sink. He still had hours to go.

"I'm going to try and take a nap. It's going to be a late night."

"If you're lucky." Nico winked.

"Not like that." Kenny rolled his eyes.

He walked down the hallway to his bedroom and laid down. He looked up at the ceiling, putting his hands behind his head. Kenny closed his eyes and tried to clear his thoughts, which was difficult, as he expected. After about thirty minutes of tossing and turning, he finally dozed off.

Later, he woke up with a start and grabbed his phone. He hadn't set an alarm and was worried he had slept too long, but it was just after midnight. He breathed a sigh of relief and peeled the covers off him. When he walked out into the hallway, the rest of the condo was dark. Nico was either out or sleeping.

Kenny walked to the bathroom and turned on the shower. He needed something to wake him up a little. Plus, he wanted to look put together for when he saw Cleo. At least, he hoped he would see her. He didn't know what to expect. She would probably be sad or angry to see him, and understandably so. He would take what he could get though.

He thought back to the last time he saw her. How happy she had looked. How in her element she was. How beautiful she looked in her chef's coat, smiling at everyone who drooled over her desserts. Then he thought back even further to when he woke up next to her that morning. She was so peaceful in her sleep. It was so hard to leave her there, when all he wanted was to pull her close and feel her breathing against him.

He started to worry that he would never feel that again. Even more so, he worried that she was giving up on her dream. Even if she wanted nothing to do with him tonight, he hoped he could convince her to stay to live out her dream.

After he was done, he turned off the shower and dried off before wrapping himself in a towel. He slid some pomade through his damp hair and put on some cologne. Back in his room, he put on his usual sweats. It was after midnight, after all. He grabbed his keys and headed out the door.

Thirty minutes later, he pulled into her driveway. He checked the time on his dash. It was 1:30 a.m. She was still working. He could have waited longer at home, but he was so antsy that he just decided to come now. He was fine with waiting though. Just being at her house gave him comfort. Plus, he didn't want to miss her.

He switched off the ignition and leaned back in the driver's seat. He drummed his fingertips on the steering wheel as he looked up at her house. Even though she wasn't due back for another hour or so, his heart was still beating faster than normal. His nerves were kicking in. He hadn't felt this nervous in a really long time.

He hadn't felt much at all in a while. Not since Sylvie. He had warded off relationships and anything remotely serious with women for years. After their relationship had ended, he had only wanted to protect himself. She was his first love. His high school sweetheart. It was hard to bounce back from that.

When he had made it to the big leagues a few years after their breakup, Sylvie had reached out to him, texted him out of the blue, which took him off guard. She told him she had ended things with her boss and that she had made a big mistake. Kenny had a funny feeling that her sudden change of heart was because of the big contract he had signed.

Still, he agreed to have dinner with her to catch up. He told her to pick the place. She ended up choosing one of the most popular places in the city for celebrities and athletes. When he picked her up, she was decked out to the nines. When they got out of his car at valet, the usual paparazzi must have thought they were celebrities, and she put on a show. He knew right then and there that she didn't want him for the right reasons. They had one drink at the bar before he left her there.

Cleo was nothing like Sylvie. She was a good person with a big heart, and she had a strong work ethic, which he admired. She didn't know much about him or baseball. He doubted she knew anything about his contract or paycheck. He knew that didn't interest her. She was different. Not just from Sylvie, but from anyone he'd met over the years. It took him messing up to realize it. Now, all he wanted was for her to be back in his life. So there he sat, waiting anxiously to see if he could convince her to be.

Chapter 27

Cleo

The bar had been packed all night, which was surprising since there wasn't a game on. Cleo barely had a moment to think through the whole night, which she honestly didn't mind. Some things were better not to be thought about. At least she felt reassured that the team or anyone associated with them was not welcome for the time being. At least until she had her last shift.

When she had quit a few days ago, she had done it so abruptly. She had been rash, which really wasn't like her. It had eaten away at her the entire next day, so she called Bridget to apologize. She also gave her a proper two weeks' notice in order for her to find a replacement. As much as she didn't think she'd be back in this place, the familiarity was comforting. In two weeks, she would head back home to Indiana and leave all of this behind.

"It's finally starting to slow down." Bridget leaned against the counter, letting out a tired sigh as they watched a large group exit the bar.

"I can't believe how busy it was tonight," said Cleo.

"Thank you again for being here. I know you want to get the hell out of this place, but I appreciate you sticking around until I find a replacement. Although, no one could truly replace you."

Cleo looked around the bar forlornly. She had so many memories here. Yes, it was just a bartending job, but this place had become her second home. It had been her first job since moving to the city. Bridget and the rest of the staff had become her family. There were a lot of customers she would miss too. She felt herself getting teary-eyed, but blinked the tears back. Bridget must have seen because she put her hand gently over hers.

"Are you sure you don't want to stay?"

Cleo shook her head quickly, swallowing her feelings down before she could change her mind. "No, I have to go."

"I understand." Bridget gave her hand a squeeze.

"Whatever happened with that creep?"

Cleo sucked in a breath just thinking about Kev's lips on hers, his hands crushing hers. It was like he had left an invisible burn on her that stung just thinking about it.

"If you don't want to talk about it, I totally get it."

"No, it's okay. They kicked him off the team. No questions asked."

Bridget smiled. "Wow! Good for the owner, and good riddance."

Cleo gave a weak smile. She thought back to when Jonas and Mae had come to her house to check on her. They were good people. She appreciated what they had done for her. Thinking back on how she kicked them out of her house, she felt guilty. The look on Mae's face was hard to forget. However, she had to do it. She didn't need anyone making it harder to leave than it already was.

Which was why she never texted or called Kenny back. She had thought about it, especially after hearing what he had done for her. While she wasn't for physical violence, that creep got what he deserved and she didn't feel guilty for thinking so. Kenny had taken up for her at the risk of losing his job. His dream.

Still, she couldn't bring herself to contact him to say thank you. She couldn't risk opening that door back up again. A text message might have turned into a conversation, which might have turned into a phone call. Hearing his voice would break all her resolve. And heaven forbid if she saw him again, it would be all over. No, it was better to just leave it be.

Cleo's thoughts must have been playing out on her face because Bridget looked at her, concerned. "You look wiped. Why don't you head out?"

Cleo glanced at the clock on the wall. "It's not closing time yet."

"Just about. Go. I can handle closing up."

Cleo gave Bridget a hug, squeezing her tightly. "Thank you."

She pulled away and glanced around the bar to be sure. It had died down a lot. There were only a handful of customers. Feeling better, she pushed through the doors to the kitchen and took her apron off, tossing it in the laundry bin. She gave a little wave to the cooks, who were playing cards and waiting for their shift to end. They gave her warm smiles and went back to their game.

The drive home went by slowly, at least it felt that way because she was so tired. It had been a whirlwind of a few weeks. Her life had completely changed since Kenny had come into it. As much as she wanted to place the blame solely on him for turning her life upside down, she knew that wasn't fair. It was him and the people in his world. In this city. As big as Boston was, it wouldn't be easy to avoid seeing him in a place that worshiped him.

She turned down her street just as her eyes began to droop with sleepiness. She couldn't wait to lie down in bed and drift off into a deep sleep. She hadn't gotten a good night's rest in a while. Too many nightmares that were very close to her reality kept waking her with a start.

She was so tired tonight, she hoped she wouldn't dream at all.

As she pulled into her driveway, her tiredness transformed into alertness. There was a car there. She felt a slight panic. She slowly drove past the car and realized she knew the black sports car—Kenny's car. Suddenly, she felt her face flush with heat. She felt angry. Why was no one getting the hint?

She slammed her thumb against the garage door opener and waited impatiently for it to open. As soon as she put the car in park, she grabbed the keys from the ignition and quickly got out of the car. She slammed her door harder than necessary, and probably a little more than her old car could handle. Seeing him was exactly what she didn't want. She had to remain firm.

She stormed toward his car and peered in the window. He was asleep. She banged her fist against the glass, waking him with a start. He blinked a couple of times as if trying to process where he was. He glanced up to see her towering over him. His eyes grew wide as he fumbled with the door handle. He finally pushed open the door, stumbling out, half asleep.

Before he could get a word out or even stand up straight, Cleo jabbed a finger in his chest. "Why can't you just leave me the hell alone?"

"Cleo, please. I just want to talk. You have to hear me out."

"I don't have to do anything!" Cleo's voice rose.

"Please. Just give me a chance." Kenny's eyebrows furrowed and there was sadness in his eyes. He didn't get to be sad.

Cleo looked over his shoulder to avoid eye contact, letting out a frustrated sigh. Maybe she was tired from a long night at the bar, or maybe she was just tired of pushing these people away, but she felt her resolve dissipate. Her shoulders slumped in defeat as she turned and walked toward her house, nodding for him to follow.

Inside, she sat in her armchair, giving him no chance or room to be close to her. He looked disappointed as he sat across from her on the couch. He looked at her warily, but she looked at the wall. She eyed him carefully from the side. He wore his sweats—her favorite—and his hair was all tousled from his nap in the car. Why did he always have to look so effortlessly good?

"Sorry to just show up like this."

"It wouldn't be the first time," said Cleo sarcastically.

"I just had to talk to you. You weren't answering any of my texts or calls."

"Why do you think that is?" Cleo looked at him sharply, crossing her arms.

"Look, I know I made a mistake leaving you here that morning. I've regretted it every day. After the night we had…"

"You didn't even call. You just left a note and then pretended like nothing ever happened."

Kenny looked down at his lap and interlaced his fingers nervously. "I know. I'm sorry for that. I was just—"

"Look, I don't really care. I don't need your excuses."

"But—"

Cleo held up her hand and Kenny stopped talking. He bit his lip as if to stop the words from coming out. She glanced quickly at his mouth, but abruptly tore her gaze away. No. She would not let herself get swept up in him no matter how remorseful he seemed. She took a deep breath and looked down at her feet. Now was her chance to say thank you and be done.

"Look, I heard what you did. What happened with Kev," she said softly.

"After you left the party so quickly, I kept trying to figure out why."

"Oh, the party where you actively avoided me? I'm surprised you even noticed I was gone."

He looked at her sadly. "I'm sorry. Okay?"

Cleo rolled her eyes and waited for him to continue.

"Well, I finally put it all together and Kev admitted it to me. I was so angry I couldn't even think straight. I just saw red. And, well, you know the rest."

"Thank you, but you didn't have to do that."

Kenny started to say something, but stopped. Instead, he stayed quiet and just looked sheepishly down at his hands. She saw that they were red and bruised, which made her stomach sick with concern, but she pushed it away. Anger replaced it. Here he was again not saying anything. She was growing tired of this. She was just tired in general.

Cleo stood slowly from the armchair and crossed her arms as she looked down at him on the couch. He looked so lost, but she reminded herself that it wasn't her job to help find him.

"I think you should go."

Kenny looked up at her with hurt in his eyes.

She hated to see him that way, so she looked away. "Please, just go. You people don't get it."

"Us people?"

"Yes! You, your boss, his wife. You just come in and out of my life as you please, even when I ask you not to. Well, I'm sick of it." Cleo tried hard not to yell.

He looked up at her, his brow raised at her tone.

She ran her hands through her hair, trying to calm down. "I appreciate what you did. Okay?

Now, can you please just go?" Her voice started to tremble.

Kenny gave her a single, slow nod and rose from the couch. He put his hands in his pockets and looked at her. This time, she didn't look away, but she refused to let herself falter. After a silent moment, he took a step toward her. She wanted to take a step back, but remained steady where she was.

He reached his hand out and tucked a piece of hair behind her ear. She flinched slightly and looked away, not because of him, but because of her memories of Kev. Kenny's eyes looked like pools of sadness and anger as he quickly pulled his hand back in retreat. As if he understood.

"I'm sorry. I know I fucked up. You and me. Us. I'm sorry, Cleo."

Cleo swallowed hard. This was all she had wanted, but it was too late now. It took everything in her to look up and into his big brown eyes.

"There was no us, Kenny. You got what you wanted from me. Why you chose me, I'll never understand. We are from completely different worlds. Maybe I was just a funny little experiment to you. Whatever it was, I'm done. I'm done waiting for you." She broke her gaze and turned away from him.

Chapter 28

Kenny

Kenny stood in silence in Cleo's living room. He looked at her standing turned away from him, her shoulders slumped in defeat. As strong as she was being in putting him in his place, as she should, he could see how drained she was. He could see it in her eyes and hear it in her voice, and it was breaking him. What broke him most was how she had flinched at his touch. He knew better than to assume it was solely because of him. As much as he hated it, he knew it was because of what Kev did to her.

In this moment, this was not the girl he had met a few months ago. She was no longer the girl who served him drinks at the bar, with no interest in who he or his teammates were. She had just seen him for him. Everyone equal, as it should be. She was kind and shy, and not wary of anyone's intentions. Now she was wary of everyone.

She was no longer the hopeful baker with dreams that seemed sky high to her because she didn't give herself enough credit. She was humble in her work, even though everyone praised her. Now she was giving it all up.

She was no longer the girl who looked at him in that way. The way that made his insides feel like they were floating. The way that was unsure of herself and only made him want to prove just how worthy she was. Now she looked at him with hurt.

He needed to get her back. Not for his sake, but for hers. He couldn't help but feel responsible for her losing herself. He had introduced her to his world and the people in it. While most were good, all it took was one to tarnish everything.

Coming here had been difficult, but he knew it wasn't a mistake. As difficult as this was and as much distance as she was putting between them, it was all worth it to see her. It was worth it to try, even though things weren't looking good at the moment. She wanted him to leave, but it was the last thing he wanted to do. He never wanted to leave her again.

He could grant her wish and walk out the door if he thought that was what she truly wanted, but there was still a small hope in him. Despite her tough exterior, there was something in the way she looked at him that told him that it wasn't over. Walking away now would be hard. She would move back to Indiana and he would probably never see her again. It pained him to think about it, but he would move on eventually.

Maybe. Probably not. A small part of him would always hold a piece of her in his heart.

As hard as it would be to walk out that door and never talk to her again, it was still the easier option out of the two he had. The other option was to stay and fight for her. For them. To open up in a way he never had in years. Tell her about his past. Fully let her in. He shut his eyes tightly as he considered the second option.

The thought of opening his heart again and cracking himself open to share the vulnerability within was scary as hell. He did not want to get hurt again, but he knew he would regret it if he didn't tell her the truth. He knew his time of standing in this house was running out.

He watched as she started for the stairs. It wasn't an invitation. It was time for him to leave. She placed her hand on the banister and took one step up.

Kenny took in a deep breath. "I had a fiancée once," he blurted out.

He watched as she paused on the stairs, but didn't turn around. He continued anyway.

"Her name was Sylvie. She was my high school sweetheart. The love of my life, or so I thought. I was young. When you're young, it all seems so easy. So pure. So clear."

He watched as Cleo's shoulders rose as she took in a deep breath. She remained frozen on the stairs, her back still facing him. At least she was listening. He would take what he could get.

"We were going to get married. We talked about our wedding and all our plans for the future. Then, in college, she took an internship across the country. We promised each other we would make it work. And we did. For a short while."

Cleo's hand gripped the banister tighter and then loosened as she listened quietly.

"When her birthday rolled around, I flew to California to surprise her. I was so excited to see her. I had it all planned in my head. I imagined the look on her face when she opened the door. My heart was so full. I was so blinded by what I thought we were that I saw past the unanswered texts and the fewer calls from the weeks before."

Kenny swallowed hard as he remembered how high his hopes had been on that flight, on the drive to her apartment, on the stairs up to it. He hadn't thought about the details in so long, it was hard to keep it together. But he knew he had to keep going. Maybe it wouldn't fix things, but maybe it would explain why he was the way he was. He cleared his throat because he could feel his voice start to tremble.

"When I got to her apartment, I knocked on the door and was met by an older man. I thought there had been some mistake. Maybe I had the wrong apartment. But then I heard her voice, and I saw her. The way she looked at me was earth shattering. She looked shocked, scared, and disgusted. All mixed together in a painful cocktail. I'll never forget that look.

"Turned out, he was her boss. Married with kids. It was all so messy. It knocked the air straight out of me. I just ran. I ran out down the hallway with them both gaping at me from the doorway. I went straight back to the airport and flew home. All I got was a text saying we were so young and she was scared to miss out on life. Something like that.

"We didn't talk again until a few years later. When I had gotten signed to the major leagues, she reached out. She was the last person I expected to hear from again. She said she had made a mistake. That she had left her boss and wanted to make things work. That we had too much of a past to give up on. A small part of me had always hoped she would come back to me one day, so I agreed to see her when she came in town.

"Except when we reunited, I didn't even recognize her anymore. Sure, she looked the same. Maybe a few years older, but inside was rotten. She was more concerned with dollar signs and fancy restaurants and being *seen.* She didn't want me. She wanted the lifestyle. She wasn't the girl I grew up with. She wasn't the girl I had fallen in love with.

"You see, infidelity seems to be a theme in my life. I recently found out that I have a brother. He was actually at that party. It's all been so complicated lately. Our father wanted nothing to do with me because I was his illegitimate son. He had fooled my mother into thinking she was the only one, but he was full-blown married with a son and a reputation he cherished more than being an actual father.

"My mother never asked for a goddamn penny from that man. He even offered a hefty sum for her to keep her mouth shut, which she did. But she did it for free. She was too proud. She raised me on her own, working multiple jobs to make sure I had everything I needed. When I became old enough to realize the sacrifices she made for me, I vowed that I would become successful on my own. I would prove I didn't need my father, and I would take care of my mother as she had taken care of me. And then some.

"I threw myself into baseball to make that dream come true. I also did it to stay distracted and closed off from love. I wanted nothing to do with it. I swore I would stay away from it, but... Cleo, I wasn't expecting you."

He let out a deep breath after the hell of a monologue he had just delivered to her. He hadn't expected to lay everything out there, especially the part about his father and his long-lost brother. But once he started, it was hard to stop. It felt good to let it all out. Terrifying, but good. Now, at least, she knew everything.

His feet shifted nervously as he waited. Kenny studied her just in case it would be the last time he saw her. He wondered if she would ever turn around. As if reading his thoughts, she turned around and stepped down, letting go of the banister. He saw tears falling from her eyes and onto her rosy cheeks. He wondered how long she had been crying for. Seeing her this way was almost too much to bear. He wanted to rush to her and take her in his arms, but he stayed put as she looked at him sadly. He didn't want to see her flinch again, not at his touch.

He took a single, slow step toward her.

"I know I'm damaged goods, but I can't let that be an excuse anymore. I don't want to continue letting my messed up past ruin my future."

Cleo watched him warily as he took another step and moved closer. She wiped the tears from her eyes with the back of her hand.

Kenny was now right in front of her and looked at her intently. "I know I fucked this up. Please let me fix this. I want you. I want *us* more than you know. That night we had together. Here. It was the best night of my life. I shouldn't have left you like that, that morning. If you give me a chance, I won't ever leave you again," he continued. He didn't take another step. He wanted her to make the next move, but only if she wanted to.

He stood patiently, watching her as she chewed on her cheek. She was deep in thought while looking at the floor. He didn't know how this would end. If this was the last time he would see her, he wanted to take her all in. Her long chestnut hair that fell in waves at her shoulders. Her fair, soft skin. Her rosy cheeks. Her plump lips. Her dark brown eyes. Her curves that she tried to hide most of the time. Her beauty.

He stood up straighter as she took a step toward him and looked up at him as if bracing himself for what would come next. He felt a little relief to see her eyes soften as she saw the hopefulness in his.

"So…exactly how rich are you?" She cocked her head and raised an eyebrow.

Her question took him off guard for a second until he saw her face break into a smile. She started to laugh through her tears. Kenny looked down at her smile and let out a relieved laugh. She *would* make a joke at a time like this. He grabbed her cheeks and bent down to kiss her. Over and over again, he quickly kissed her lips, her cheeks, her forehead. And she let him, laughing and crying tears of happiness all the while.

Chapter 29

Cleo

Cleo couldn't help but laugh as Kenny covered her face in kisses. Now, instead of crying tears of sadness, they were turning to tears of happiness. She never thought he would be here again, let alone kissing her. She kept her eyes shut tight as his lips brushed quickly against her eyelids and onto her cheeks. She had never seen this side of him before. This playful and affectionate side.

She had also not seen the side of him that he shared so personally. The hurt she heard in his voice as he recounted his past was too much to bear. She had kept her back turned because if she were to have seen his face, it would have broken her. Cleo had no idea of his past, and now she knew everything. It felt like she was let into some secret club where there were very few members, and she felt grateful for the pieces he shared with her.

She couldn't imagine someone hurting him the way his ex had. Cleo silently cursed her for messing with his heart so carelessly. On top of all that, he had a father who had practically shunned him. What Kenny had been through was so far from anything she had been through in life. It made sense as to why he could be closed off, even though it had broken her heart. What was she to expect from someone whose heart had been dropped so many times?

Kenny stopped kissing her and she opened her eyes to look up at him. He had a soft smile on his lips as his eyes studied her face. His palms felt warm against her cheeks. God, he was handsome. She bit her lip expectantly as she waited for his next move. He trailed his thumb across her cheek and down to her lip, pulling it from her teeth. She kissed his fingers slowly.

He closed his eyes and took a deep breath before opening them again quickly. There was a diffcrent look to him now. A lustfulness in his warm brown eyes. She felt it wash over her, and the skin on the back of her neck prickled. Before she knew it, his hands were in her hair and his lips were on hers. Her mouth parted to allow his searching tongue to find hers and mesh together. She moved her hands up to his head and her fingers tangled in his unruly hair.

She desperately needed him closer as their tongues massaged against each other. She pulled him toward her and he gladly followed until her back hit the banister of the stairs. He pressed his body against hers. She could feel him growing hard against her. It made her feel powerful. It made her feel incredibly sexy. It made her wet.

Cleo untangled her fingers from his hair and moved her hands to his strong chest. Kenny's mouth left hers and traveled to her neck. He kissed her along her collarbone before trailing his tongue up just below her jaw and up to her earlobe. She shuddered at the sensation. Her hands trailed down his hard stomach and she grazed her fingertips against his growing erection. He looked down at her hungrily. She smiled up at him as she massaged her palm against him. He shook his head at her as she teased him through his sweats.

"Do you even know what you do to me?" he asked breathlessly.

She shook her head slowly, looking up at him, feeling him grow harder in her hand.

Suddenly, as if he couldn't take it anymore, he picked her up and she wrapped her legs around his waist. She squealed with delight as he headed up the stairs. She tried not to think about how much she weighed, but he walked up the steps with ease. His muscles against her felt hot. Stupidly hot.

He carried her to her bedroom, gently swinging the door open with his foot. Her arms clutched his neck as he swiftly walked to her bed. He set her down so she was standing at the edge of the bed, facing him as he towered over her. He looked as if he didn't know where to start. She looked at him coyly, wondering what his next move would be.

He moved his hands to the hem of her shirt and pulled it up and off, revealing her large breasts that sat cupped by her black lace bra. He looked at her admiringly as his hands cupped her breasts, squeezing them gently. She could feel her nipples growing hard against his palms. Feeling them hard against him, he kneaded them between his fingertips gently. She leaned her head back and arched her back with pleasure.

She felt his warm breath against her breasts as his hand traveled to her back, unhooking her bra. It fell to the floor as her breasts spilled out before him. She lifted her head and looked at him. His eyes were taking her in, and soon his mouth was wet against her breast. Kenny's tongue swirled against one nipple before moving to the next. His eyes were on her the whole time. *Holy fuck. This is hot.*

Cleo ran her hands through his hair as he continued kissing her breasts, sucking and licking her supple skin. She couldn't take much more of this and moved her hands to his neck and pulled him down to the bed with her. She lay against the plush mattress as he propped his arms up on either side of her. Kenny bent down and ran his tongue against her breasts again before moving lower. His lips and breath brushed against her stomach, causing her breath to hitch.

She propped herself up on her elbows for a better view. He watched her as he continued moving his mouth down, stopping at the waistband of her jeans. He unbuttoned them and grabbed her hips, lifting them up as he pulled on her jeans. He shimmied them off and tossed them aside as she lowered her hips back down to the bed.

His gaze moved over her entire body. Instead of feeling self-conscious, she felt wanted. She enjoyed every second of it. She wanted to see him too. She sat up slowly and tugged at the hem of his sweatshirt.

"My turn," she said, looking up at him.

He let out a little laugh as he pulled his sweatshirt up and over his head, revealing his six pack. Her eyes took in his chest, his abs, his V. She leaned back and admired him. This man wanted her. Why? She didn't know, but she sure as hell could get off on the way he looked at her.

He climbed on to the bed, his eyes never leaving hers. He lay on his side as he faced her. She turned her face toward him and he kissed her softly, running his tongue over her lips. She felt his hand graze against her thigh, his fingers barely touching her as they moved upward. Her skin broke out in goosebumps. Then his fingers were against her panties. They moved lightly against her. Cleo lifted her hips to meet his hand needily. He applied a little more pressure, massaging against the lace of her panties. She could feel herself wet against him.

Kenny pressed against her as he continued kissing her, his tongue moving in sync with his fingers. His hand created a delicious friction against the lace of her panties. She moaned into his mouth. She wanted more. She needed it. He got the message. Kenny grabbed her panties and pulled them to the side. He dipped a finger into her with ease, causing her to let out another moan. He pulled his finger slowly out of her, swirling his palm against her clit before dipping his finger back in.

She struggled to hold it together. She wanted to orgasm with him inside her, filling her, but it felt so good. But she was hungry for more. She shimmied her hips away from him, and moved away from his searching fingers. She pushed him onto his back roughly, taking him by surprise. A good surprise. Kenny watched as she slid her panties off and climbed toward him. She lowered herself onto him, straddling him. His sweats were still on, but that didn't stop her from grinding against him. She watched as he watched her rub herself against him slowly.

"Fuck. Cleo."

She bit her lip as she pressed her hands against his chest, continuing to move against him. When she was close to the edge, she lifted herself off him and tugged at the waistband of his sweats. She pulled them off quickly as his erection jutted out. She sucked in a breath just looking at it. Cleo lowered herself so her mouth was just inches away and looked at him as she licked her lips before placing them on the tip of his shaft. She parted them slightly, taking him in inch by inch. His eyes rolled back in his head as she ran her tongue under the base. She began moving her mouth up and down in a slow rhythm, feeling him tense in her mouth.

She continued sucking and stroking him until his hands were in her hair, pulling her toward him. She eased her mouth from him and looked at him expectantly.

"I need you now," Kenny said desperately.

She climbed up his body, hovering over him. He lifted up and kissed her passionately. Then his hands were on her hips, his fingers digging into her plump skin and positioning her on top of him. She could feel the tip of his erection against her, and she felt herself tense and then open. She lowered herself onto him slowly, feeling just the tip of him slide inside her with ease, before lifting her hips. He looked up at her pleadingly.

Cleo smiled as she swirled her wet slit around the tip of his erection before eventually lowering herself a little more than last time. She lifted herself up again, feeling herself growing wetter and him growing harder. His hands reached for her hips again, grabbing them tightly. She was no longer in control now. She braced herself as he lifted his hips and pushed her down onto him, filling her completely. She let out a loud moan of pure pleasure. He slammed into her again, filling her even more. He kept pushing her onto him until they were both at their peaks.

When they were both breathless, he slowed his movements, but maintained his grip on her hips. He moved her against him, grinding her deeper on to him. He was hitting her just so, causing her fingers to dig into his chest as she threw her head back and moved rhythmically against him. She felt Kenny tense inside of her as she completely let go, exploding around him. He let out a moan as he gripped her tighter before letting her go as she fell on top of him in a breathless heap.

She cradled her head under his neck as their breathing slowed. She ran her fingers across his chest and smiled to herself. How was that even better than the first time? Kenny kissed the top of her head and sighed.

"I could definitely get used to this," he whispered.

"Mmm."

"If you'll let me, of course."

She lifted her head and looked at him. He looked a little sad.

"I'm so sorry for everything, Cleo." He shook his head.

"It's okay. I know you are." She looked at him intently. She knew this was eating away at him, but she didn't want it to.

"I'm not going to leave you again." He traced her face with his fingertip.

"I know," she said. And she did. She knew he was it for her, and that he felt the same about her.

"Does this mean you're staying in Boston?" he asked.

"I'm staying," she said.

He leaned in and kissed her.

Chapter 30

Cleo

Kenny gave Cleo a kiss on the cheek before getting out of the car and walking to her side to open the door for her. Before she got out, she looked up and smiled at him. She still couldn't get over how good-looking he was, especially when in a suit. His deep brown eyes filled her with a pool of warmth. He reached his hand out and helped her out of the car. He guided her inside the large glass doors of the building.

They waited for the elevator to reach the lobby floor and Kenny tapped his foot quickly, creating a rhythm against the marble floors.

"Sorry we're late," said Cleo, squeezing his hand.

"No biggie. It was worth it." Kenny winked at her and she felt herself blush.

They seemed to be late for everything these days. It was hard for them to leave home. A home that was now collectively theirs since he had asked her to move in with him a few weeks ago. It had taken her by surprise because they'd only been together for five months, but when he brought her coffee in that morning, there was a key on the saucer next to the mug. He had looked at her nervously, but she gave him a resounding yes without him even asking the question. He almost spilled the coffee when she pulled him into bed excitedly.

It was perfect timing. She was coming up on the lease ending at her house, and Nico had been looking for his own place for some time. He was happy for them. They weren't the only ones moving. Justin had just moved back to the city, much to Kenny's excitement. That's why they were here at this brand-new building of luxury condos. Justin was having his housewarming party.

The elevator dinged and the doors opened. They were greeted warmly by the doorman.

"Floor?" he asked, his finger hovering over the buttons.

"Penthouse, please," said Kenny as he led Cleo to the back of the large elevator. He leaned casually against the railing, but was eyeing Cleo mischievously. She raised a questioning eyebrow as she looked up at him.

As the elevator started its ascent to the top floor, Cleo felt Kenny's hand trailing slowly up her backside, lifting the back of her flowy dress with ease. He looked straight on, as if nothing was happening, but everything was happening inside of her. He always made her feel wanted, and she always wanted him. His hand cupped her bottom and his fingers trailed the edges of her lace panties. She shook her head at him playfully, eyeing the doorman. Kenny grinned down at her before giving her a little squeeze. She would take him right here in this elevator if it weren't for the unaware old man standing in front of them.

In the months they had been together, they could not keep their hands off one another. It was as if they were exploring uncharted territory, and no space could be left undiscovered. This was the reason they were late all the time. Their friends had become used to it, saying they were in the honeymoon stage. Obviously, they weren't married yet, but Cleo thought about it. Often. It was early into their relationship, but when you know you know.

The elevator slowly came to a stop and Kenny slid his hand from beneath her dress.

"The penthouse," the doorman announced.

The doors slid open to reveal 360-degree views of the city below, framed by large white pillars and freshly polished, dark wood floors.

"Justin does not mess around," said Cleo, looking around in awe.

"You've got that right." Kenny smiled as he grabbed her hand, nodding at the doorman as they exited the elevator.

The party was in full swing with jazz music playing, cocktail tables spread throughout the room with crisp, white tablecloths, and champagne and appetizers being served on trays. For how many people were here, the room did not feel crowded at all, which spoke to its size.

"Glad you two could make it." Justin approached, giving them a wink.

"Sorry we're late," said Kenny.

Justin gave him a knowing look and a pat on the back before turning to Cleo and giving her a big hug.

"This place is amazing," said Cleo, looking around the large room.

"Thank you. I've spent the past few months designing it. I still can't believe I'm in Boston now."

"It took some convincing," said Kenny, giving his friend a little jab in the shoulder.

Justin let out a laugh. "Let's get you some drinks. The bar is this way."

"You two go on ahead. I have to get the pastries from the car. I forgot them there in my rush. "

"You made pastries?" asked Justin excitedly. "You didn't have to do that."

"You know I love to," said Cleo.

After thinking it over, she had decided to not give up on her dream of owning her own bakery in the city. Business had been booming, especially with the help of Mae's birthday party. She knew it would be stupid to throw away those contacts and all that business. These were good people, and she wouldn't let what happened with Kev ruin that. That would mean he had won, and she was stronger than that.

She had been working out of the kitchen at their condo, which was double the size of her old kitchen. Still, she had even been outgrowing the condo kitchen. It was almost time to rent a space of her own, which Kenny had been encouraging her to do. He was so supportive. He loved her passion, which she appreciated so much.

"I'll help you," said Kenny.

"I can help!" Mae walked up and gave Cleo a warm hug.

"Are you sure?" Kenny looked between them.

"Go. Have a drink. I'll be back before you know it." Cleo waved him off.

Justin and Kenny walked to the elegant bar that sat in the corner of the room. Cleo watched him for a moment. She wondered if she would ever get over the butterflies. Probably not.

"Look at you. So in love," said Mae with a smile.

"Is it that obvious?" asked Cleo, tearing her gaze away from Kenny.

"Couldn't be more obvious. I'm so happy for you two."

Cleo smiled at Mae. They had become close friends in recent months. After Cleo decided to stay in Boston, she had made amends with Mae and Jonas. She had apologized for how she had treated them both after everything that had happened with Kev. They were more than understanding and were thrilled to hear that she was staying. Soon after they made amends, Mae had her baby, a beautiful girl named Lily.

"Where's Lily tonight?" asked Cleo as they headed toward the elevator.

"She's with Jonas's mom. She came to town to visit. She's obsessed with Lily. It's the cutest thing."

"Aww. That's so sweet."

They rode the elevator down and Mae updated her on all of Lily's recent milestones. Cleo loved to see her friend so happy and so in tune with motherhood. She was made for it. Down at the car, Cleo popped the trunk and pulled out a large pastry box. She handed it carefully to Mae, and grabbed the other one before closing the trunk.

"What did you make this time?" said Mae eagerly.

"Eclairs, mini cappuccino cheesecakes, chocolate pistachio mousse towers, and lemon Chantilly cake," said Cleo proudly. "Kenny even helped out."

She smiled as she thought back to them working together in the kitchen, his arms around her as she mixed and poured. He would read off the recipes to her, his lips close to her ear. They took quite a few breaks, but they eventually finished.

"You're blushing," said Mae, looking at her amused.

"Need any help?"

Cleo turned and saw Elle approaching them. She wore a form-fitting black dress and her hair was pulled back into a slick ponytail.

"Elle! You look fantastic," said Cleo, as she gave her a side hug, trying to balance the pastries.

"Thank you." Elle did a little twirl.

Cleo smiled at her friend. She was happy to see her so confident. After her breakup with Brad a few months ago, which was her idea, Elle had felt a little lost. It was the best decision for her because she felt like they had drifted into more friend territory. She said it felt like they were just roommates. It was heartbreaking for her, but she eventually found her way.

"I think we've got it, but thank you," said Cleo as they headed back inside. The doorman held the door as they made their way to the elevators.

As they rode up, the three of them enjoyed their girl talk. Elle quickly filled them in on who she was talking to lately. Since she had been coming around to more of the baseball games with Cleo, there were a few players who had their eye on her. She was enjoying the attention.

When the elevator doors opened to the party, Elle was immediately approached by Nico, as if he sensed she was nearby. Mae and Cleo giggled as they nudged Elle on their way to find the kitchen. It wasn't hard to miss with how gigantic it was. They began plating the pastries onto serving trays for the waiters to pass out later in the evening.

"These look and smell fantastic," said Mae.

"Thank you," said Cleo.

"You know, Jonas is looking to invest in some smaller companies around the city."

"Mhmm." Cleo finished one tray and moved to the next.

"He was thinking a bakery…"

"Mmm."

"Cleo, are you hearing what I'm saying?"

Cleo paused what she was doing and looked up at Mae, as if just then processing what she had heard. Mae looked at her with a big smile, which reassured her that she had heard right. They wanted to invest in her?

"Do you mean…?"

Mae nodded enthusiastically. "You're amazing at what you do. We know you'd become a city hotspot. We would just be investors. Everything else would be up to you. Your vision."

Cleo couldn't find the words. Her eyes started welling up with tears, but she blinked them back quickly. "Mae, I don't know what to say."

"I know it's a lot. But just promise you'll think about it."

Cleo suddenly gave Mae a huge hug. "Thank you."

Mae hugged her back tightly. Just then her phone rang. She pulled away and searched her purse for her phone. "It's Jonas's mom. I have to take this. She said she'd call around bedtime so I could say goodnight."

"Okay. Tell Lily hi!"

Cleo watched Mae walk out of the kitchen and then let out a deep breath. She couldn't believe her dream was going to come true. Of course, there was a lot to still figure out and she wouldn't accept their offer unless she knew she could make it a successful business that would pay them back and then some.

She finished plating the final tray and walked dreamily out of the kitchen and back into the party. She saw Kenny leaning against a pillar, holding two glasses of champagne. When he spotted her, he beamed and signaled for her to come over. She felt like she was floating as she made her way through the party. His eyes on her made her feel like she was the only one in the room.

He handed her a glass of champagne and pulled her close to him, kissing her gently on the forehead. She rested her head against his chest, listening to his heartbeat. This was a whole new life for Cleo. She had a famous boyfriend. She was interested in baseball now. Instead of serving drinks at Murphy's, she sat at the booth with Kenny and his teammates. She no longer needed two jobs because her baking business took off and she was about to take the next big step. None of this would have happened if she had run back to Indiana. Plus, there probably wouldn't be a hot baseball player there to sweep her off her feet.

Epilogue

Kenny

Kenny stood with his hand on the door, ready to enter the bakery, but he stopped at the sight of Cleo through the window. Her hair was pulled into a loose bun and she wore her pink chef coat. Her smile was beaming as she filled the pastry case with fresh muffins. He didn't think she could get more beautiful, but seeing her doing what she loved proved him wrong.

She had only opened her bakery a few months ago, but it had already become a hot spot in Boston. Everyone was talking about Cleo's. The papers all had rave reviews and popular bloggers had shared photos of the pastries and the bakery itself, which was just as charming as Cleo's culinary creations.

Cleo had found the perfect corner spot on a popular street to rent. After giving it a great deal of thought, and a lot of persuasion from Kenny, she had agreed to let Jonas and Mae be investors, at least until she got her footing. And boy, had she.

She must have felt his gaze because she spotted him through the window and waved for him to come inside, her smile growing even bigger. He pushed open the door and took in a deep breath. The air was filled with the sweet smells of cake baking. He licked his lips as he looked around the bakery. Every table was full of customers enjoying their morning coffee and pastries.

Cleo wiped her hands on a towel before she approached him from behind the counter. He wrapped his arms around her, pulling her close before giving her a soft kiss on the lips. She smelled like blueberry muffins. He loved that about her. He could always count on her smelling like dessert.

"This is a surprise," she said.

"I had a little time to kill before heading to the airport to meet the team."

"Mmm. I'm going to miss you, you know."

"I think you'll be too busy running the most popular bakery in the city to miss me."

She turned and looked around the bakery as if having a pinch-me moment. She leaned back and lay her head against his chest.

"I sometimes can't believe it," she whispered.

"Well, believe it," replied Kenny.

He wrapped his hands around her and placed them gently on her growing belly. It had been a few months since she had told him she was pregnant. They had been standing in this very bakery before it had opened and become what it was now. It was the happiest moment of his life.

As excited as she was, Kenny knew she was a little scared to be embarking on motherhood and her own business. He did everything he could to reassure her every day because he believed in her. Because she was worthy of someone believing in her full force. Because she was the mother of their baby boy. Because he loved her.

He planned on letting her know just how much as soon as he got back from his away game. With a solitaire diamond ring.

This is the end of Kenny and Cleo's love story.

Want to be notified when the next book in the series featuring Bridget and Justin is released?

Or would you like to read a free romance novel from me instead?

For both, click here and subscribe:
https://BookHip.com/LHLBBPG